Praise for

Mr. Malcolm's List

"Allain's writing is wry and delightful."

—*Entertainment Weekly*

"Suzanne Allain delivers a fresh and spirited take on the classic Regency romp. *Mr. Malcolm's List* is a delightful tale that perfectly illustrates the enduring appeal of the Regency romance. It's all here—the fast, witty banter; the elegant ballrooms; the quirky characters; the charming, strong-willed heroine; and the dashing hero who has a thing or two to learn about love."

—*New York Times* bestselling author Amanda Quick

"A merry romp! *Mr. Malcolm's List* is packed with action as one tangled romantic misunderstanding follows fast upon another's heels—to hilarious effect."

—*New York Times* bestselling author Mary Balogh

"Suzanne Allain is a fresh new voice in historical romance. *Mr. Malcolm's List* is a charming, lighthearted confection, with humor, sparkling banter, and gently simmering romantic tension; in other words, classic Regency romance."

—National bestselling author Anne Gracie

"Allain's characters are witty and appealing, and the sizzle between Jeremy and Selina is convincing. This effervescent love story is a charme̶ ̶ ̶ ̶ ̶ ̶ ̶ ̶ ̶*hers Weekly*

D1014306

"[This] captivating Regency is sure to be oft-requested and relished by fans of the period."   —*Library Journal*

"Hilarious and fast-paced, *Mr. Malcolm's List* is a bright and refreshing Regency romp."   —Shelf Awareness

"A cheeky look at the different expectations placed on men versus women during the Regency era, revealing the limitations society accords individuals in terms of their family connections and personal wealth and education. Both general fiction readers and romance fans looking for a story that will transport them to another time and place, seeking new fictional friends, or hoping to watch characters grow more self-aware and compassionate will revel in this smart love story."   —*Booklist* (starred review)

"It was witty, hilarious, and contained a cast of upbeat, brooding, and feisty characters that all graced the page with subtle [*Pride and Prejudice*] undertones. I loved it!"   —The Nerd Daily

Titles by Suzanne Allain

Mr. Malcolm's List
Miss Lattimore's Letter

Miss Lattimore's Letter

SUZANNE ALLAIN

Jove
New York

A JOVE BOOK
Published by Berkley
An imprint of Penguin Random House LLC
penguinrandomhouse.com

Library of Congress Cataloging-in-Publication Data

Names: Allain, Suzanne, author.
Title: Miss Lattimore's letter / Suzanne Allain.
Description: New York : Jove, [2021]
Identifiers: LCCN 2021008722 (print) | LCCN 2021008723 (ebook) |
ISBN 9780593197424 (trade paperback) | ISBN 9780593197431 (ebook)
Classification: LCC PS3601.L398 M57 2021 (print) |
LCC PS3601.L398 (ebook) | DDC 813/.6--dc23
LC record available at https://lccn.loc.gov/2021008722
LC ebook record available at https://lccn.loc.gov/2021008723

Printed in the United States of America
1st Printing

Book design by Daniel Brount

For my sisters

1

It had been many years since Sophronia Lattimore had used her fan as a means of flirtatious communication. As a poor relation of eight-and-twenty, she was now too firmly ensconced amongst the chaperones to try to attract a gentleman's attention, but if one *had* noticed the frantic waving of her fan he could have no doubt of the message it was sending: Sophie was desperately overheated. And she was not the only lady so afflicted. Odors of perfume and perspiration mingled in the warm air, causing Sophie to feel so stifled she determined she must escape into the cool night if she were to maintain consciousness. Thankfully her cousin had just joined a set, so Sophie had some time before Cecilia would be looking for her.

She made her way around the perimeter of the overcrowded ballroom toward the French doors she'd espied across the room and went through them onto a narrow balcony. She walked to the opposite end, away from the light of the ballroom, and took in some brisk, refreshing breaths. Lost in quiet contemplation of the night sky, she was startled when a couple came out of the ballroom onto the balcony. Before she could make her presence known—as she still stood in the shadows and they had not noticed her—they hurried into speech.

"What exactly are you about, Priscilla?" the gentleman asked.

"I don't know what you mean."

"Do not play games with me. It's quite obvious you're encouraging Lord Fitzwalter's suit. Do your promises mean nothing?"

"Of course they do. And you will always have my heart, Charles, you must believe that! But I was only taking my own feelings into account, and I've since come to understand my family must be considered as well." She put out her hand in a pleading gesture. "Please, Charles, you cannot hold me to those promises. I was too young."

"Or you've begun to envision yourself a countess."

"You must realize I never expected, or even desired, to capture his notice, but now that I have, my mother—oh, what's the use of speaking. You cannot possibly understand—"

"I think I understand all too clearly."

The gentleman turned and left; the lady, whom Sophie had recognized as Miss Priscilla Hammond, followed a moment later.

Alone again on the balcony, Sophie reflected on what she'd unintentionally heard. Miss Hammond's first London season had been an indubitable success, with Lord Fitzwalter at the forefront of the numerous gentlemen paying her court. That he was on the verge of a proposal was common knowledge, and the lady's acceptance was also a foregone conclusion. After all, what young woman from an undistinguished family of moderate means would turn down the opportunity to become a wealthy countess? But apparently Charles thought that Miss Hammond might do so, in his favor.

Sophie returned to her seat in the corner, still preoccupied with what she'd discovered. She sympathized with all the parties in this tangled affair. There was even a fourth person she knew to be affected: her cousin's friend, Lucy Barrett, had confided in Cecilia that *she* was enamored of Lord Fitzwalter, and was in despair over his attentions to Miss Hammond. Lucy Barrett, though an attractive young woman, hadn't enjoyed the popularity that Miss Hammond had. A trifle shy, she tended to become overwhelmed in crowds and hesitated to put herself forward. She'd only come to know Lord Fitzwalter because he was a friend of her brother.

It was a complicated business, this making of matches. And it was none of Sophie's affair if Lord Fitzwalter chose Miss Hammond over Miss Barrett. But would he really have decided upon Miss Hammond if he knew Miss Hammond and this "Charles" had made promises to each other? Was Miss Hammond merely acceding to the wishes, and perhaps the pressure, of her family?

Sophie watched Miss Hammond for the next half hour and found she did not seem like a young lady delighted by her beloved's attentions. Though she smiled at Lord Fitzwalter frequently enough, that smile just as instantly faded, replaced by a frown, as soon as his head was turned. The person who looked most pleased by Lord Fitzwalter's attentions was Mrs. Hammond, who positively gloated at the sight of her daughter with the earl.

Sophie was distracted from her thoughts by her cousin Cecilia's appearance. "Sophie, Mr. Hartwell has offered to escort me to the refreshment room."

"Would you like us to bring you a glass of punch, Miss Lattimore?" Mr. Hartwell asked.

"How kind of you. That would be lovely," Sophie replied. She would have actually preferred to accompany them and escape her uncomfortable seat, but she had no wish to disturb their tête-à-tête, even though that was ostensibly one of her responsibilities. However, her aunt really only expected Sophie to insert her unwelcome presence upon unsuitable *partis*, which Mr. Hartwell was not.

"That's a feather in your cousin's hat," an elderly lady sitting next to Sophie said in what she apparently thought was a lowered tone of voice, but which caused Sophie to look quickly toward the departing couple in hopes they had not heard. She was relieved to see they were too engrossed in their own conversation to have heard Mrs. Pratt.

"Yes, Mr. Hartwell seems like a pleasant young gentleman," Sophie said vaguely.

"Pleasant-pheasant. He's heir to an estate worth five thousand a year. Related to the Duke of Norfolk on the distaff side," Mrs. Pratt replied.

Sophie was too accustomed to Mrs. Pratt to expect anything less than a recital of a young man's income and ancestors, and little though Sophie might care about such matters, Cecilia's mother very much did, so it behooved Sophie to pay attention. And then it occurred to her that she could perhaps use Mrs. Pratt's encyclopedic knowledge of eligible gentlemen to satisfy her own curiosity. Sophie had seen Charles making his way across the ballroom and nodded her head in his direction.

"Mrs. Pratt, do you know that gentleman? I believe his Christian name is Charles."

Mrs. Pratt peered myopically across the ballroom in the direction Sophie had indicated, before reaching for the lorgnette hanging from her neck and raising it to her eyes. Sophie instantly repented of her question when Charles turned and looked directly at Mrs. Pratt, who made no secret of the fact that she was not only staring at him but using an apparatus designed to help her get a better look. Sophie started to turn away, but it was too late; Charles had noticed her as well. He looked puzzled at the attention he was receiving from the wallflower contingent but gave both ladies a slight nod before leaving the room.

"Beswick. Youngest son of Baron Fane. He's from the same parish in Devonshire as our belle of the ball, Miss Hammond," Mrs. Pratt said finally.

"So, a decent match."

"Respectable. Not the heir, of course, but he inherited a smallish estate." Mrs. Pratt dropped the lorgnette to look at her companion. "Who are you asking for? You or your charge?"

"Obviously not myself," Sophie said, attempting to evade the question.

"Why not? That aunt of yours has made you into a spinster before your time. You're still young and handsome enough to make a match. And if I were your age I know exactly who I'd set my cap for."

Now Sophie was regretting more than ever that she'd begun this conversation, because in Mrs. Pratt's excitement her voice trumpeted even louder, and people were turning to look. One of those who did, a smile on his handsome lips, was the very man to whom Mrs. Pratt referred. And Sophie did not need Mrs. Pratt to point him out to her.

No, she was very aware of Sir Edmund Winslow, as were several other ladies. He was not to be found at every social event of the season, so when he did appear it was as if some rare species of bird had lit near a waddling of ducks. His presence was as invigorating as the fresh air she'd taken on the balcony earlier; but now, meeting his eyes directly, she felt the need to remind herself to breathe.

However, she didn't cower or shyly bow her head, as she so frequently did when sitting amongst the chaperones, particularly if a gentleman looked her way. If this were her last opportunity to exchange charged glances with a personable gentleman, she decided to throw caution to the winds and take it. She sat up straighter and smiled slightly at him and was sure she saw a gleam of something—some interest, curiosity, even attraction—in his gaze. She forgot all about Mrs. Pratt, the vulture at the feast, who was observing their exchange with interest.

"See there, you've caught his eye," Mrs. Pratt announced to all and sundry. It was exceedingly awkward, and very decisively nipped any feelings of mutual attraction in the bud. Sophie did drop her eyes, but not before seeing Sir Edmund turn his head away and quicken his step. Mrs. Pratt tuttutted. "Too bad, he's gone. I would have introduced you if he'd lingered long enough."

Sophie was very conscious of the eyes and ears still turned in her direction. London society was like a fox hunt, with every member poised to start chasing at the first whiff of humiliation. Sophie was generally ignored, but if a nonentity such as she dared to aspire to a match above her station, this was a tidbit that could enliven an evening when no meatier prize was in sight. So she was relieved to see Cecilia and her escort returning with her glass of punch, which effectively ended her conversation with Mrs. Pratt.

Sophie would perhaps have forgotten the scene on the balcony, or at least disregarded it, if she hadn't been thrown into company with three of the principal players in the drama very soon thereafter. Her cousin Cecilia and Lucy Barrett were bosom friends already, and as Miss Hammond was of a similar age and circumstance to the two young ladies, the girls often found themselves invited to the same gatherings, along with Miss Hammond's suitor, Lord Fitzwalter. Of Charles Beswick, Sophie saw nothing more. She surmised he had left London rather than remain to see the object of his affections courted by another. When Sophie found herself sitting next to Priscilla Hammond at a concert a week later, she sought to assuage her curiosity.

"I wonder, Miss Hammond, if you could tell me about a neighbor of yours, a Mr. Charles Beswick. Is he still in town?"

Priscilla's eyes widened and her breath caught. "Charles? I mean . . . Mr. Beswick? He is an acquaintance of yours?"

"Not of mine, but of another lady, Mrs. Pratt. She was asking after him and mentioned that you were from the same parish."

"Oh, I see," Priscilla said, though she looked understandably confused by Sophie's interest. Sophie would not have blamed Priscilla for refusing to answer such an impertinent question, but after a moment Priscilla continued: "Mr. Beswick has returned home. I do not expect to see him again." As Priscilla's tone and expression was that of a mourner at a funeral, Sophie could only surmise that Priscilla was greatly saddened by this fact. And when she observed Lord Fitzwalter in conversation with Lucy and noticed how much happier he seemed than during his superficial exchanges with Priscilla Hammond (which consisted mostly of compliments on her appearance), she really felt that he was making a grievous mistake. This was confirmed by Cecilia, who ranted about Mrs. Hammond's manipulations, which were separating her friend Lucy from Lord Fitzwalter and blighting her future.

While Sophie realized that the situation might have been exaggerated by her younger and far more dramatic cousin, the more she observed them the more she grew to believe that Lucy was genuine in her affection for Lord Fitzwalter and that the two had already established a warm friendship, something that Sophie considered, with her limited experience, would provide a sound foundation for marriage. Lucy was of a more serious and quiet nature and did not shine in public like Priscilla Hammond, instead tending to withdraw whenever the other girl flirted with Lord Fitzwalter, so it was not surprising that Priscilla was more successful in gaining and keeping his attention. And since it appeared that Priscilla's heart was not given to Lord Fitzwalter but to someone else entirely, Sophie did feel that this was an occasion when plain speaking could perhaps avert a sad mistake. However, she really did not feel it was her place to approach Lord Fitzwalter, with whom she'd never exchanged more than pleasantries. How could she inform him that his pursuit of Miss Hammond was an error in judgment? He would rightly tell her that it was none of her affair, and she could find herself repudiated by London society. She could even lose her place with her aunt.

But what if Lord Fitzwalter was unaware of the identity of his adviser? What if she passed him a word of warning anonymously, without him discovering from whence it came? Her conscience would be clear and he would be free to act or not, relying on his own best judgment.

And so Miss Lattimore wrote a letter.

It was the talk of the town a little over a month later when Lord Fitzwalter, whom everyone expected to offer for Miss Hammond, announced his betrothal to Miss Barrett instead. No one could accuse him of ungentlemanly behavior, however, because his engagement followed the news of Miss Hammond's own betrothal to a Mr. Beswick of Devon.

Cecilia, who was sitting out a dance by her cousin's side, asked wonderingly, "Who in the world is Mr. Beswick?"

Before Sophie could respond, Mrs. Pratt piped up. "What a coincidence. Your cousin asked about that same gentleman just last month."

Cecilia looked at her cousin in surprise. "Really? What brought *him* to your notice, Sophie?"

Sophie found herself at a loss for words. She had never anticipated anyone asking her such a question and had no idea how to respond. She was not very skilled at dissembling, and it became fairly obvious to her audience that they'd stumbled upon some mystery when her eyes grew large before she averted her gaze entirely. "Idle curiosity," she finally replied.

Cecilia was palpably skeptical. Forgetting they were not alone, she incautiously said, "Lucy told me that someone wrote a letter to Lord Fitzwalter—"

"Cecilia, I do believe Mr. Hartwell is approaching," Sophie interrupted.

"Nonsense, he's dancing a reel with Miss Tibbits," Mrs. Pratt said shortly. "Continue, young lady. What is this about a letter to Lord Fitzwalter?"

Cecilia suddenly realized the danger of revealing her bosom friend's confidences in the presence of a notorious gossip. "Oh, it was nothing of interest. Merely a note of congratulations on their engagement." Cecilia, who was much more skilled at prevaricating than her older cousin and, though a decade younger, had far more practice, refused to succumb to Mrs. Pratt's probing and was happy to escape for a set with the most undistinguished gentleman she'd danced with yet.

Later, in the carriage, Cecilia turned to her cousin. "It was you who wrote the letter, was it not?"

Sophie, who could not tell a lie—or at least not very believably—nodded. "But please, Cecilia, do not tell anyone."

"It's nothing to be ashamed of, Sophie. Lucy and Lord Fitzwalter consider you did them a great favor."

Sophie could not but feel heartened that her decision to take action had been the right one and that she was receiving commendation for it. It had been so long since anyone had listened to, or even sought, her opinion. She had felt almost invisible these last six years she'd lived with her aunt after the death of her father. Cecilia was the only one who had granted her the least bit of notice or affection, but it was of the careless sort, as Cecilia was not all that interested in an older spinster cousin.

But now Cecilia was looking at Sophie with grudging respect and approval, as if some heretofore unknown talent she possessed had been revealed.

"I suppose it would do no harm for you to tell Lucy I wrote the letter," Sophie said, after a short time spent contemplating the matter.

Cecilia looked surprised that Sophie would think it was even open for debate. "But of course I shall tell her. She has been positively beside herself with curiosity since Lord Fitzwalter told her of it. And really, she has every reason to be grateful. If you had not written to him, Lord Fitzwalter would have been lost to her forever. But Cousin, people are saying you wrote in your letter that Priscilla Hammond was in love with a different gentleman. How did you know about Miss Hammond and Mr. Beswick?"

2

*S*ir Edmund sipped his weak punch and wondered why he'd come. He always felt uncomfortable at these affairs. He was careful to smile at none of the ladies who peered at him hopefully over their fans, and finally decided to get more of the flavorless punch, as it would at least remove him from the dancing.

Not that Sir Edmund didn't enjoy dancing. It had been a favorite diversion, once upon a time.

Lord Fitzwalter hailed him as he entered the refreshment room, and Sir Edmund walked over to speak to him, pleased to see someone he knew.

"I hear congratulations are in order," Sir Edmund said, once greetings had been exchanged.

"Indeed they are. You see before you the most fortunate of men."

Fitz certainly looked happy, but the last time Sir Edmund had seen him Fitz was paying court to Miss Hammond, so Sir Edmund was justifiably confused at his friend's engagement to an entirely different woman. "I don't believe I'm acquainted with your betrothed," Sir Edmund said, hoping this would prompt Fitz to offer an explanation for the change, as he had to realize Sir Edmund *was* acquainted with Miss Hammond, as Fitz was the one who had introduced them.

"That must be remedied, though you will have to meet her later. She's dancing at the moment. With Ludlow," Fitz said, nodding in that direction. Sir Edmund followed his gaze, curious to see the femme fatale who had stolen his friend's heart. He saw a very demure-looking girl who, while pretty enough, couldn't hold a candle to Priscilla Hammond. But then Miss Barrett seemed to sense their attention and glanced over at Fitz. And she smiled so sweetly and lovingly at him that Sir Edmund immediately realized how wrong he was in thinking Priscilla Hammond the more attractive choice.

Fitz shook his head in amazement. "I still cannot believe how things worked out."

"Since you've raised the subject, I find myself curious as to how this engagement *did* come about. Rumor had it you were courting an entirely different young lady."

"Rumor was correct in this instance. If it were not for the unselfish benevolence of an anonymous lady, I would have probably found myself betrothed to the wrong person altogether." Fitz hurried to add, "Of course, Miss Hammond is a lovely young woman and Beswick is to be congratulated, but Lucy . . ."

Fitz sighed and smiled in a manner Sir Edmund felt was a trifle inane, but then chided himself for being uncharitable. He probably only felt that way because he was envious of his friend's good fortune.

"An anonymous lady?" he prompted Fitzwalter.

"Well, her letter was anonymous, but she is not any longer." As even Fitz, in his deliriously happy state, realized this speech was annoyingly incoherent, he began at the beginning, telling his friend the details of Miss Lattimore's letter.

Sir Edmund listened with rapt attention, only interrupting his friend once to ask if he might be permitted to call on him and read the letter for himself. Fitz surprised him by saying he was carrying it on his person and removed it from his waistcoat pocket, handing it to his friend.

It was not a long letter, and Sir Edmund read it fairly quickly, before reading it a second time, more slowly. Fitz, who was impatient to sing the praises of his fiancée, bided his time while Sir Edmund examined the letter, but as soon as Sir Edmund handed it back to him Fitz began eagerly recounting how correct Miss Lattimore was in her assessment of Lucy's "pure and tender heart." He also told Sir Edmund how surprised he'd been to learn of Lucy's feelings for him, as he'd always been fond of her but thought she viewed him as an older brother. And while Sir

Edmund listened politely as Fitz gushed about Lucy, he soon displayed where his real interest lay.

"Who is Miss Lattimore?" he asked.

That was the question of the evening, though it took Sophie a few hours to realize her name was on nearly everyone's lips. She was holding up a wall, watching the dancing and tapping her feet under her skirts, when she began to notice more and more glances in her direction. Still, she was too modest to assume she was their object of attention, and kept looking to either side of her, expecting to find someone or something of interest. The only thing she found, and it was not the least bit interesting, was that the ubiquitous Mrs. Pratt was napping and had begun to snore.

And then Mr. Dodd asked her to dance, a request she politely refused. She had to admit to herself that for once she was happy to be sitting amongst the wallflowers, as Mr. Dodd smelled unpleasantly of garlic and his teeth reminded her of a neighbor's donkey that had bitten her when she was a child.

But then another gentleman stepped forward, and another, and eventually Mrs. Pratt was awakened by the unusual activity and began making impertinent remarks and encouraging Sophie to accept various invitations. Sophie, who could bear no more, told the most recent gentleman who had requested a dance that she must find her cousin and left her seat to scurry across the room to where Cecilia stood speaking with her friends.

But when Sophie drew near to the group she felt extremely awkward and ill at ease, as they all stopped talking and turned to look at her upon her approach.

"I beg your pardon; I've interrupted your conversation. Pray continue," she said to Lord Fitzwalter, who had paused mid-sentence.

"Miss Lattimore! We are well met," Lord Fitzwalter said, his tone of voice expressing nothing but delight. Lucy Barrett was at his side, and she, too, looked pleased to see Sophie. And then the gentleman at Lord Fitzwalter's other side looked her way.

"Sir Edmund Winslow, may I present Miss Lattimore," Lord Fitzwalter said, and Sir Edmund bowed to her.

Sophie quickly debated whether she should curtsy or merely bob her head before she did drop into a curtsy, while telling herself not to dip *too* low as if Sir Edmund were royalty. Really, her thoughts were in such a whirl she barely knew what she was doing, but she recovered somewhat when she made herself turn her gaze from Sir Edmund and focus on Lord Fitzwalter instead.

"Sir Edmund had just expressed a wish to make your acquaintance, Miss Lattimore, so your arrival is quite timely," Lord Fitzwalter said.

Sir Edmund frowned at Lord Fitzwalter before turning back to Sophie and forcing a tight-lipped smile. "Indeed, I am pleased to meet someone so highly regarded by my friend," he said.

Sophie tentatively smiled back, and Sir Edmund's expression relaxed somewhat. Sophie thought perhaps he was annoyed to have Lord Fitzwalter proclaim him eager to meet her, but she was fully aware if he had expressed such a wish it had to have been an offhand remark, made from politeness or curiosity. She knew better than to imagine he had more than a fleeting interest in her, unfortunately.

Lord Fitzwalter spoke again, this time to mention a dinner party he was planning in honor of his engagement that he hoped Sophie would attend. Sophie accepted gratefully, as this was the first invitation directed specifically to her that she could remember since she had come to live with her aunt. Any social event she attended she did so only on sufferance, a necessary but unwanted presence, her cousin or aunt being the real recipient of the invitation.

However, Sophie soon found that things had changed.

Invitations for Sophie flooded the small town house in Leicester Square, and with each one Sophie's stature seemed to rise in the eyes of her aunt and cousin. Her aunt had never been cruel to her, but as Sophie was the daughter of her husband's sister and no blood relation of her own, she had made it very plain that Sophie could never expect more than a roof over her head and a seat at her table. Sophie had a small allowance left to her by her father, but it was only enough to cover the barest of essentials, and without her aunt's charity, grudging as it was, she'd be in sore straits indeed. So even though Sophie prayed for her aunt Foster each day, thanking God for her aunt's generosity in taking her in, the words came much more readily and sincerely when her aunt looked at Sophie with a smile rather than a frown.

Sophie's relationship with her cousin had also improved, but she was unsure if this was something to rejoice over or bemoan. Cecilia would now visit Sophie's bedchamber almost every night before bed, desirous of knowing her opinion of her suitors. As it was Sophie's opinion that Cecilia should wait a good deal longer before contemplating marriage, she found the conversations about each beau's merits and deficits a trifle tedious, but she was grateful that her cousin at least sought her counsel. And she was even more grateful that Cecilia, who had heretofore left Sophie to dress herself, had offered her the services of her maid Betsy to assist with her hair.

Sophie gladly left off the alterations in her attire that she had made so as to appear as inconspicuous as possible and mute any natural attractions she possessed. She had begun doing so at the start of the London season when she'd taken on her role as chaperone, in an attempt to make her status more obvious. Though her aunt had not explicitly told her what to wear, she had told Sophie how imperative it was that she present a "mature appearance, in keeping with her age and position." But now that her aunt was encouraging Sophie to accept invitations on her own behalf and not as Cecilia's unacknowledged escort, Sophie put all of her caps in a drawer and stopped covering her shoulders and décolletage with shawls and lace fichus. Thus, her aunt and cousin began to wonder if she had always been as handsome as she now appeared and they had not noticed, or if her newfound popularity was causing a latent bloom.

Cecilia took after her mother, tall and fair-haired with blue eyes, while Sophie was slighter with dark hair and gray eyes. Cecilia had always thought her cousin, older and smaller as she was, to be the quintessential old maid, long past any prospect of attracting a gentleman's notice. It was to Cecilia's credit that she felt pleased rather than threatened by her belated discovery of Sophie's attributes.

Of course, Cecilia and Mrs. Foster's pleasure was not entirely, or even primarily, on Sophie's behalf. Both could not help but reflect on how Sophie's sudden social success could benefit *them*.

The Fosters occupied a position on the fringes of high society, and while they were solidly genteel and distantly related to more than half-a-dozen respectable and even noble families, their fortune was modest, something that both ladies planned to remedy by Cecilia's imminent marriage to a gentleman of fortune. She had at least attracted one such suitor since her debut, Mr. Hartwell, but he was only a plain mister and it was early days yet. (And Cecilia considered him somewhat dull and unexciting.) It was her aunt Foster's hope that through Sophie's increased social activity Cecilia would be exposed to even more eligible gentlemen than her modest come-out had afforded her the opportunity to meet thus far. And if there was an aging widower or a respectable clergyman willing to marry Sophie, well, that would only be to the good, taking her off of her aunt's hands.

Since there was not even the remotest possibility that Sophie would make a match *superior* to that of her younger cousin, it was just as well that this vexatious thought did not enter into her relations' conjectures.

Sophie, who had wondered why she had caught the fancy of London society, was not left to wonder long. Those who sought her company usually did not come to the point straightaway, pretending instead an interest in her friendship or company, but it was eventually made clear that they thought Sophie had some unique talent for matchmaking and wished to secure her services for themselves. She even discovered from her cousin that she'd earned the sobriquet "Lady Cupid."

Sophie was able to politely put off most of those who desired her assistance, as they were usually too diffident to pursue the matter, but she was genuinely astounded when she found Sir Edmund was one of that number.

She had seen him at Lord Fitzwalter's dinner party, though they had had no opportunity to converse beyond the barest civilities. But she found herself very shortly thereafter in company with him again on an excursion to Strawberry Hill.

The outing had been planned and executed by Lord Fitzwalter, who wanted everyone to share in his happiness and so was hosting more activities than he ever had before. The weather matched his mood, as it was a beautiful June day, sunny with a refreshing breeze. After a tour of the house, the party picnicked on the grounds on the banks of the Thames. Sophie had never visited Strawberry Hill, the house and gardens designed by Horace Walpole, the famous Gothic novelist, and she had never before been on a picnic, either. At least, not a picnic such as this, in the company of other ladies and gentlemen. After lunch she walked the paths lined by rosebushes full of buds and blooms and felt such joy, along with a conviction that this was to be the summer of *her* life, her season to blossom. Then she laughed inwardly at herself. She had felt this way once before when she was Cecilia's age, and had discovered herself to be sadly mistaken. She should know better than to hope for too much, or to trust her own frequently self-delusory instincts.

She didn't even trust herself as far as her attraction to Sir Edmund was concerned. She really knew nothing of him beyond his handsome appearance, and Sophie had learned the hard way that a man's good looks, far from being a measure of his character, were indicative of nothing more than a happy accident of birth. And even if Sir Edmund were a man of sterling character, there was very little hope he would be interested in an impoverished spinster like herself.

Still, when he appeared at her side as she walked, she could not completely control her quiver of excitement at his presence. But when she discovered his true purpose in seeking her out, she tried to console herself with the knowledge that things had occurred precisely as she had foretold and that she had been a wise woman to temper her expectations.

The conversation was casual at first, Sir Edmund merely inquiring which part of the country she'd come from and asking about the length of her acquaintance with Lord Fitzwalter and Lucy Barrett. But then he introduced the subject he'd apparently approached her to discuss. "I have heard that you played a part in bringing about this engagement."

"Perhaps a small part," Sophie replied, not wanting to sound boastful but knowing it would look like false modesty if she denied it when Lord Fitzwalter apparently was telling any- and everyone.

"Have you always had a talent for this sort of thing? How did you know the two couples would suit?"

"I have no special talent; it was just based on observation. Indeed, I do not claim to be skilled at making matches. I very much doubt I'll ever do so again."

"Will you not? But you've made at least two people very happy."

Sir Edmund gestured to where Lord Fitzwalter was sitting on a bench in conversation with Lucy. They did appear incandescently blissful, and Sophie had already noticed that they could not stop smiling or looking at each other. While Sophie and Sir Edmund watched, Lord Fitzwalter brought Lucy's hand to his lips and tenderly kissed it. Sophie felt guilty to be observing them during such an intimate moment and looked away, quickening her pace until there was a turn in the path and she could no longer see the couple. Sir Edmund followed, adjusting his step to hers.

"I am more pleased than I can say that they are so happy," Sophie said, once they were again strolling slowly. "I really did very little, and I was always conscious of the fact that I could unintentionally cause more harm than good." She shook her head. "Truly, it is a responsibility I do not desire."

"But do you not think, especially in genteel society where a couple go into marriage knowing very little of each other, that your assistance could be of great benefit? A gentleman cannot spend a great deal of time in observation or conversation with a prospective bride, lest he be accused of trifling with her affections and be forced into a marriage to suit convention, rather than himself."

Sir Edmund had stopped walking and turned to face Sophie, and so she did likewise. She wondered that he did not recognize what he'd just said could also apply to *their* situation. They were separated from the rest of their party in a sheltered part of the gardens, in earnest conversation with each other. If anyone saw them, they risked censure and gossip. But perhaps Sir Edmund felt that Sophie's age, lack of wealth, and role as chaperone excluded her from such considerations. How old was *he*? she asked herself. Surely he was at least her age, if not a few years older. She wondered that he had not married by now. And what it was he wanted from her.

"What is it you are suggesting, Sir Edmund?" Sophie asked.

Sir Edmund smiled, a little wryly. "I'm not sure, really. I'm a hypocrite, I suppose. Here I am accusing you of keeping your talents to yourself and really all I desire is your help in securing *my* happiness."

"You desire to marry?" Sophie asked, trying to appear as if his answer mattered little to her.

"Of course. I am a single gentleman in possession of a good fortune, so I must be in want of a wife."

Sophie smiled at his reference to the popular novel written by "a lady" that she had also read and enjoyed. But she didn't really feel like smiling. She felt like she was cursed, destined always to watch others pair off while she remained alone. And lonely.

"And do you have a particular lady in mind?" Sophie forced herself to ask, though she had absolutely no desire to hear Sir Edmund praise some other woman.

"No, I do not. Unfortunately, there are no Elizabeth Bennets to be found in my home parish."

"Is Lizzy Bennet your ideal, then?" Sophie asked.

"Of course. A woman of wit and good sense, determined to marry not for advantage but for affection. She is precisely who I am looking for."

Sophie shook her head in mock despair. "But Sir Edmund, therein lies your problem: she doesn't exist."

"There must surely be ladies like her, however. Look at you," he said, gesturing vaguely at her. Sophie felt the weight of his gaze as he took in her appearance, and she hoped he found nothing to criticize. "I am certain, when you wrote Fitzwalter that letter, you had no thoughts of the size of his fortune when recommending Miss Barrett to his notice."

"You are correct. I did, however, think of Mr. Beswick's," Sophie said with a smile.

"I do not understand."

"I knew that Miss Hammond's mother *was* swayed by material considerations, and I felt that she would not allow her daughter's match if Mr. Beswick had no prospects at all. So I inquired into his circumstances before writing the letter."

Sir Edmund smiled warmly at her. "A woman with her wits about her indeed. But we should probably return to the others," he said, looking around him as if wondering how they'd ended up in so isolated a situation. "Your cousin will be looking for you."

Cecilia *was* looking for her cousin, but not because she desired her company. No, she had seen her walking with Sir Edmund and had determined to join them. However, before she could do so, Mr. Hartwell had approached her, and in conversation with him she had lost sight of Sophie and Sir Edmund.

Cecilia felt Mr. Hartwell's attentions were becoming a little irksome and thought perhaps it was because of him that she was unable to attract a more desirable suitor. Still, a bird in the hand was worth two in the bush, and she was hesitant to discourage him *too* much. It was rather gratifying to have a gentleman rush to one's side to request a dance, offer to fetch a drink, or put his carriage at her and her cousin's disposal, as he had this very day.

She just wished he were older and more sophisticated and less blond and cherubic. That instead of his honest, open, slightly bulbous blue-eyed gaze, he would look at her from glinting dark eyes. She wished he were . . . Sir Edmund Winslow.

But when Sophie and Sir Edmund returned from their walk, Sir Edmund merely nodded at Cecilia and said: "Here is your cousin, Miss Foster. I am sorry to have kept her from you." He then turned to leave almost immediately, before Cecilia had time to do more than offer a smile and a "Thank you, Sir Edmund."

She was excited to see him approach again just as she and Sophie were about to get into Mr. Hartwell's carriage to leave. But Cecilia could not flatter herself that Sir Edmund even noticed her presence. He merely asked Sophie if she would drive with him the next day and, at Sophie's surprised acceptance of his invitation, asked for her direction. He wished Cecilia a good day and left as quickly as he'd come.

Cecilia, noticing again how attractive Sophie appeared and that her cheeks were tinged with pink, had a moment's regret she'd lent her Betsy to do her hair.

3

*S*ophie's aunt Foster had no doubt Sir Edmund's attentions to Sophie would eventually result in his
taking notice of Cecilia. Particularly since she instructed
her niece to ensure they did so.

"Sir Edmund Winslow very rarely comes to town, pre-
ferring instead to spend much of his time at his estate in
Somerset," Sophie's aunt told her. "And while he is merely
a baronet, there are very few eligible members of the peerage resident in London this season." She interrupted herself to tsk in disdain. "It's too bad Lucy Barrett snatched up
Lord Fitzpatrick so quickly. You know, Sophronia, you might
have mentioned *Cecilia* in your letter to him rather than
Lucy, a girl to whom you're not even related." As Sophie
didn't know how to respond to this accusation, and even
Cecilia looked as if she were about to protest, Mrs. Foster

didn't allow them a chance to speak. She continued, "But that cannot be remedied, so it appears as if Sir Edmund is our best prospect. You must take advantage of this rare opportunity, Sophronia, to recommend your cousin to his notice as often as the conversation permits you to do so."

Cecilia quickly spoke up. "Mama, if Sophie were to do as you say, it might become too obvious and have the opposite effect from what you intend." She turned to address Sophie. "You must not mention me *so* frequently, Sophie, that he becomes suspicious. But if you are able to subtly insert my name into conversation, you could then learn what opinion he holds of me."

Sophie inwardly rebelled against such an order, vowing to herself that if Cecilia's name even crossed Sir Edmund's lips, she'd turn the subject immediately. However, then Cecilia smiled very sweetly at her and said: "But I trust you to follow your own counsel in this matter. I know you have my best interests at heart."

Sophie, feeling ashamed of her ungenerous thoughts toward her cousin, could only manage to smile and nod, though she had no clear idea to what she was agreeing.

However, when Sir Edmund arrived he did not enter the Fosters' town house, as Cecilia had hoped he might, merely sending his groom to tell their manservant he was waiting for Miss Lattimore outside. He did, though, hand the reins to the boy and jump down to help Sophie into the curricle himself.

It had been ten years since Sophie had ridden with a gentleman in a curricle, and she was a little overwhelmed at first by the sensations crowding in on her. The feelings had begun when Sir Edmund lightly clasped her hand and waist as he helped her onto the seat, and were intensified when he sat beside her, just a scant few inches away. The smell, sight, and sound of the horses, the wind in her hair, the sun on her cheek; all of her senses were alive and tingling, and she silently instructed herself to somehow make a record of this moment in her brain so she could relive it in the weeks, months, and years to come.

She had no wish to make idle conversation and could think of nothing to say anyway, so the drive passed in near silence until they entered the park and Sir Edmund slowed the horses. He then turned to her with a smile. "Lovely day, is it not?"

"Absolutely beautiful. I'm so glad the temperate weather has continued to hold," she replied, smiling back at him. In their smiles and glances she felt they were both expressing much more than their mundane words implied; that he, too, felt this was a golden moment in time, to be appreciated and treasured.

"I'm grateful you agreed to drive out with me. I am leaving town but wanted an opportunity to speak to you again before I did so."

How quickly a cloud could roll in and the warm breeze turn chill! "I am sorry to hear you are leaving, Sir Edmund. Your friends will miss you; especially Lord Fitzwalter," Sophie said, and congratulated herself that she sounded only mildly disappointed, as befitted the departure of a casual acquaintance.

"To tell you the truth, Miss Lattimore, I'm not convinced Fitz would even notice I'd left," he said. "He's quite occupied with his future bride at the moment, as he should be. But I have promised to stay for the wedding, at least."

There was a momentary interruption as an acquaintance drove by and he and Sir Edmund exchanged greetings.

"Where do you go?" Sophie asked, and then wondered if he would think such a question impertinent.

"To my estate, Newbrooke, in Somerset. My steward has written me; there's some problem between two of the tenant farmers. He probably could handle the matter himself, but it seems like a good excuse to return home."

"You are not a fan of the London season, Sir Edmund?"

"I am not comfortable around strangers, no," he said.

He exchanged nods with a gentleman in another passing carriage.

"But it appears that you have many friends in town," Sophie said.

"I know a great many gentlemen, it is true. I number fewer ladies among my acquaintance."

"Since you have expressed a desire to marry, it would seem you need to enlarge your circle of acquaintances," Sophie said.

"That is precisely why I invited you to drive with me this afternoon, Miss Lattimore," he said, before apparently realizing his words might be construed as meaning he saw *her* as a potential bride. "I beg your pardon, I did not mean—

I meant, I invited you in order to request your advice on how to become better acquainted with a lady, without creating unfulfilled expectations if I should find we do not suit."

"Is it your desire to protect the heart of this hypothetical lady or your own?" Sophie asked, impelled by the pang of her own remembered foolishness that summer she was eighteen.

Sir Edmund turned to look at her, and Sophie wondered if it was merely her pain she saw reflected back to her, or if he had suffered similarly. "Both," he replied. "I have no desire to wound anyone, nor do I want to suffer heartache myself. I don't mean to make it sound, however, as if I rate myself so highly that I think ladies will be tumbling into love with me," he said with a self-deprecating smile, and Sophie felt a sudden responsibility to her sisterhood, as Sir Edmund looked so sublimely handsome at that moment and obviously had no notion of how much of a threat he actually was.

"If you want my counsel it is this: widen your circle of acquaintances, without paying marked attentions to any particular lady. If one does catch your fancy, observe her in group settings and see how she interacts with others. Choose with your head first, before involving your heart."

Sir Edmund did not reply for a moment, reflecting on her words. "It sounds like a prudent course of action."

Sophie suddenly grinned, lightening the serious mood that had descended upon them. "That is what my name means, you know."

"Your name?" he asked.

"Sophronia. It means sensible or prudent."

"Sophronia," Sir Edmund repeated softly, and Sophie felt anything but sensible. "'Tis a pretty name."

Sophie lowered her eyes, wondering how she was so imprudent that she had somehow just granted him the intimacy of using her Christian name.

Before Sir Edmund returned Sophie to her home, she asked him how far he lived from Bath.

"Very near, actually. No more than ten miles."

"Had you thought of attending the assemblies there?" she said.

"Do you suggest I do so?"

"I doubt you will meet many eligible young ladies in dealings with your estate manager or tenant farmers."

Sir Edmund sighed. "You are right, of course. Where do you and your cousin go at the end of the season?"

"My cousin?" Sophie asked, wondering at his introduction of Cecilia into the conversation. Perhaps he *was* interested in her, after all.

"You live with her and her mother, do you not? I assume if you leave town you will do so together?"

"Yes, but we have no plans, as of now, to leave town."

"I've recently had Bath recommended to me as a desirable destination," he said with a half smile.

"An inspired suggestion," Sophie replied. "I'll mention it to my aunt."

Sophie was merely jesting when she said she'd mention a stay in Bath to her aunt, as she had no intention of chasing Sir Edmund around England. After all, he gave no indication that he saw her as anything more than some kind of sexless mentor and dispenser of sage advice. Most certainly he did not view her as a woman, the type of woman he was concerned with wounding with his attentions. (That didn't prevent Sophie from admiring him for his sensitivity toward this yet-to-be-discovered lady and even envying her.) She found it far easier, however, to bid him luck in his quest for true love and put him out of her mind. She had absolutely no desire to watch him court the object of his desire.

But she found when she returned home that her aunt and cousin somehow misconstrued the information she relayed about her drive as an invitation to join Sir Edmund in Bath. The confusion came about when Cecilia asked if Sir Edmund had mentioned her.

"Once. He asked where we are to go after the season ends," Sophie replied, and could have bitten off her tongue when she saw that she had somehow encouraged her aunt and cousin in their delusions.

"Upon my word, that is a promising sign!" Mrs. Foster said, with a fond look at her daughter. Cecilia appeared gratified as well, and Sophie wondered how she could have so unintentionally misled them. "Did he say where he goes?"

"To his estate," Sophie said, determined to offer only the briefest of answers to their queries.

"Where exactly is it?" When Sophie did not respond quickly enough, Cecilia turned to her mother. "Do you know, Mama?" she asked.

"In Somerset, very near to Bath," Mrs. Foster told her daughter, before turning to Sophie. "Did he say whether he plans to attend any of the assemblies there, Sophronia?"

Sophie wished she didn't have to answer. She reluctantly said, "He mentioned he *might*. I do not think he has made definite plans."

Her aunt spent a moment in thoughtful silence before announcing her decision. "We shall take a house in Bath for the summer."

"Bath!" Cecilia exclaimed, twirling around in glee. "How delightful! Are you not excited, Cousin?" she asked Sophie, whom Cecilia couldn't help but notice was not responding in like manner (but then she was very dizzy and may have misread Sophie's expression).

"'Excited' does not begin to describe my feelings," Sophie replied.

However, Sophie eventually did find herself growing excited at the prospect of removing to Bath. She'd never been before, as after her father's death she'd gone directly to London from her home near Tunbridge Wells, which was also a spa town. Her father would never have thought to take her to Bath when there was a similar, though less modish, option so near. She'd always wished to travel but until now had contented herself with doing so through the pages of a book. Yet here was an unexpected opportunity to explore a city that was famous for its architecture and entertainments, and she remembered her prediction that this summer was to be special and wondered if this was proof that she'd been quite astute.

But before they could leave for Bath there were a few social engagements they could not miss, one of them being the wedding of Lord Fitzwalter and Miss Barrett—or Lucy, as Sophie had now been given permission to call her.

It was held at ten on a Friday morning at St. George's in Hanover Square, and there was likely to be at least one ceremony before and after, as St. George's was quite busy that time of year. Sophie wondered that the vicar performed the reading with such enthusiasm, as he had probably recited it a hundred times at least. Sophie herself felt the solemnization ceremony was distinctly *too* solemn at times, especially the part that seemed to amount to an accusation of criminal behavior on the part of the bride and groom. She thought this vicar, a relation of Lord Fitzwalter, might agree with her, as he seemed to speed up as he recited the words:

"I require and charge you both, as you will answer at the dreadful day of judgment when the secrets of all hearts shall be disclosed, that if either of you know any impediment why you may not be lawfully joined together in matrimony, ye do now confess it."

Sophie felt that if she were ever to marry she would hope for a clergyman like this to officiate, as she had sat through very long and awkward pauses at other weddings, where the participants (and witnesses) had been the target of accusing stares before the vicar proceeded with the ceremony, and the words "dreadful day of judgment" had been spoken in highly significant tones. But this vicar passed over that part of the reading as quickly and lightly as possible, barely pausing for a reply, slowing again when he asked Lord Fitzwalter if he would have Lucy "to thy wedded wife." He even appeared, wonder of wonders, to be *happy* for the bride and groom.

Sophie, as delighted as she was for Lucy and Lord Fitzwalter, had one niggling source of discontent. Cecilia was one of the attendants, along with Sir Edmund, and Sophie found the sight of them at the altar somewhat hard to bear, even though the bride and groom stood between them. She told herself that if Sir Edmund were to court Cecilia she should rid herself of her silly infatuation and be pleased for them both, but the thought of having to be an eyewitness to every aspect of the affair, as well as having to serve as Cecilia's confidant, was more than a little daunting. She greatly wished that Sir Edmund would find some other young lady to pursue, and quickly, and that Cecilia would find it in her heart to accept the more than admirable Mr. Hartwell.

Mr. Hartwell was present as well, peering soulfully at Cecilia, who deserved every one of his admiring glances, as she was looking quite pretty, while still doing her very best to fulfill her first duty as bridesmaid: not to eclipse the bride in beauty.

There was a wedding breakfast served at Lord Fitzwalter's town house after the ceremony, and Sophie had been invited to it as well. There she was able to become further acquainted with Mr. Hartwell, to find him even more obliging than she had previously thought him, and to wonder that Cecilia did not marry him straightaway before some other lady took advantage of her dillydallying.

Mr. Hartwell had learned from Cecilia that she, Mrs. Foster, and Sophie were to repair to Bath for some months and he had immediately requested the privilege of assisting them with their travel arrangements, putting his own carriage at their disposal and providing them with his escort.

"For I, too, find the thought of an excursion to Bath at this time of year quite a refreshing prospect," he told Sophie, though he looked a little sheepish as he said this, and Sophie had no doubt he'd think an excursion to Tasmania a refreshing prospect if that's where Cecilia were headed.

Sophie had given herself a stern lecture between the church and the wedding banquet and convinced herself that she had no interest in Sir Edmund at all beyond the natural concern one would have for the dear friend of a friend. She even smiled beguilingly at an uncle of Lucy's, but after he sought her out she soon found herself regretting the impulse. Mr. Barrett was a member of the Jockey Club with a tidy bit of property in Leicester, and Sophie found herself learning far more than she'd ever desired to know about the Newmarket races, the Atherstone Hunt, and a Squire Osbaldeston, who was apparently the "best dashed cricketer and master of the hunt to ever be born of woman." (Since Sophie knew of no other way for a man to be born, she assumed this meant he was quite literally the best.)

So it was difficult for her to hide her relief when Sir Edmund approached them, and in consequence she greeted him far more warmly than she'd intended. Mr. Barrett, presented with evidence that Sophie was very liberal with her smiles and thus no better than a coquette, took himself off and found a fellow sportsman (in the library of all places) who gave him a good tip on the July races.

"I had no idea you were a devotee of equestrian sports," Sir Edmund said to Sophie, once Mr. Barrett was out of earshot.

"I am not; and have learned quite enough today to satisfy any ignorance I had on the subject."

"So you would not be interested in a description of the chestnut I picked up at Tattersall's; a prime bit of blood and bone, got by Blackleg out of Sprightly? I plan to run him at Newmarket."

"Do you, indeed?" Sophie asked, curious about this insight into his personality. She had not thought him one of the Corinthian set.

"I do, actually, but we do not have to discuss it. I'd prefer to hear about your plan to remove to Bath."

Sophie was a little embarrassed at this reminder, thinking he must believe her to be pursuing him there, but she could detect nothing satirical or knowing in his direct and friendly gaze. "Cecilia told you, I suppose," she finally said.

"Yes, and I am quite happy that you took me up on my suggestion. She says Mr. Hartwell is helping to arrange matters."

They both looked across the room to where Cecilia stood talking to Mr. Hartwell. "Yes," Sophie said. "Mr. Hartwell has been very obliging indeed."

"I imagine it is to be a match between them?" Sir Edmund asked, lowering his voice.

Sophie looked up at him, alarmed. "Oh, no; matters have not yet reached that stage. It is premature to speak of it." She wondered at her eagerness to proclaim Cecilia available and unattached, but she felt it would be unfair somehow to eliminate her as a rival based on a false belief, and Sophie refused to stoop so low.

"But it would be a very good match, and there appears to be genuine affection between them, on his side at least. I wonder that you do not use your talents to promote it," Sir Edmund said, his brow furrowed in confusion at her negative reaction.

"I could not interfere in my cousin's affairs. I must allow her to make her own decisions."

Sir Edmund shook his head. "I shall never understand you, Miss Lattimore. Here we are, at the wedding celebration of a match *you* instigated, and yet you appear to have an aversion to making matches."

"It is not an aversion, it is just . . . a profound respect, I suppose, for the institution. You were at the ceremony today. It is a wonder that any mortal enters the bonds of matrimony when it is announced at the outset that it is not to be taken 'unadvisedly, lightly, or wantonly, but reverently, discreetly, advisedly, soberly, and in the fear of God.'"

"I think you left out a portion," Sir Edmund said, with a wicked twinkle in his eye. And Sophie, who had knowingly omitted the part about how marriage should not be undertaken to "satisfy men's carnal lusts and appetites," had a difficult time keeping a straight countenance and could not prevent a blush from warming her cheeks.

There was a slight pause and then they both began laughing.

"Trust the church to expound on matters not to be mentioned in polite society," Sir Edmund said.

"And to ascribe the basest of motives to human behavior," Sophie added.

Sir Edmund opened his mouth to reply, stopped himself, and merely shrugged. Sophie was left to wonder if he disapproved of her implied criticism of the church, or if he disagreed that such motives for marriage were base. She could not think too deeply on the second supposition and remain comfortable in his presence, so she was relieved when he spoke again.

"To return to the subject of your trip to Bath, have you found a house to let?"

"We did, with Mr. Hartwell's help. It is on Rivers Street," she said.

"An excellent address. Mr. Hartwell is to be commended. May I call on you there?"

Sophie was surprised but attempted to conceal it by answering calmly: "Yes, of course. We'd be very pleased to receive you."

4

The remove to Bath took place as smoothly as could be desired. (Which is to say, Sophie, Cecilia, and Mr. Hartwell were not discomposed in the least, but Mrs. Foster found a thousand things to trouble her.) Sophie felt more strongly than ever that Cecilia would be a fool to reject so good-natured and accommodating a young gentleman as Mr. Hartwell, who was also pleasant in appearance and quite sensible. But she realized those qualities did not rate very highly to a young lady of eight-and-ten.

Sophie felt that if Mr. Hartwell had not appeared at the very start of Cecilia's come-out and so quickly made obvious his admiration for her, things would have transpired very differently. Little did Cecilia know—when her knowledge of gentlemen was so scant—that to win the favor of a gentleman like Mr. Hartwell was quite an achievement. It was Sophie's opinion that because it had come so early Cecilia tended to undervalue his regard and wonder if she could do better. Sophie could understand her thinking but could not approve of it. She felt very uncomfortable that Mr. Hartwell was taking on many of the duties of a husband with little assurance that he would ever achieve that position, and with only fleeting and faint smiles from Cecilia as a reward. In consequence, Sophie found herself smiling at Mr. Hartwell more than ever.

But then, Sophie found herself with a smile on her face most of the time, these days. No place she'd ever seen delighted her more than Bath (though it was true she had not seen many places). Still, she felt even if she were to one day visit Paris or Rome, or some other grand city, Bath would still hold a special place in her heart. She infinitely preferred living there to living in London.

Sophie had purchased a copy of *The Bath Guide* at a local bookshop, and while she had no doubt its author was somewhat biased, especially when asserting Bath to be "one of the most agreeable, as well as one of the most polite places in the kingdom," she did concur that a lot of its charm was "owing to the elegance of its buildings, which are superior to any other city in England." In the previous century, two architects, a father and son both named John Wood, designed and constructed buildings of a warm, honey-colored stone that was now ubiquitous in Bath. Sophie's favorites among their designs were the Circus and the Royal Crescent, rows of narrow town houses that were curved into circular shapes and mimicked the Colosseum in Rome, but turned inside out.

Then there were the hot springs which gave Bath its name. Legend had it that they were initially discovered in the ninth century before Christ by a leprous prince named Bladud. Bladud had been shunned at court because of his loathsome disease and had become a lowly swineherd. But this proved to be his salvation, as the pigs, who had caught his leprosy, rolled in the warm mud of the hot springs near Bath and were cured. This led Bladud to also bathe in the miraculous waters, which cured him of his disease and enabled him to be restored to the throne. Sophie was not surprised, however, to find that her trusty guidebook labeled this legend "a fabulous and absurd tale."

However, a man who did live up to the legend was Richard "Beau" Nash, the dandy who had reigned supreme over Bath society as master of ceremonies in the previous century. He was revered in Bath, and a statue of him peered condescendingly from a niche above the Pump Room at the people who flocked to drink the famous waters. It was a mystery to Sophie why the man had allowed so many artists to paint his portrait and sculpt his figure when the likenesses were not at all flattering, and displayed the bags under his eyes and the unhealthy color of his complexion, as well as his multiple chins, in graphic detail. Sophie would have thought that these would be the worst possible advertisements for the supposed health benefits of Bath, as the famous Beau appeared a very unhealthy specimen indeed.

The Pump Room itself, though, was definitely one of Bath's aesthetic treasures, despite Beau Nash's likeness being displayed prominently on its walls. Situated adjacent to the King's Bath, it had been rebuilt in 1796 to replace a smaller building, and every morning it filled with hundreds of people of all ages (but mostly the elderly) who had come to drink the medicinal waters that were pumped from the hot springs into a marble urn in an enclosure behind a bar. However, it was also the place to see and be seen, and ladies and gentlemen would stroll up and down the brightly lit room with its many windows and high ceilings suspended above Corinthian columns, chattering loudly over the noise of the orchestra.

And then there were the assembly rooms, the Abbey Church, Sydney Gardens, and the natural beauty of the hills that surrounded Bath and the river that flowed through it. Truly, Sophie found much to feed her soul and spirit; far more than she'd found cooped up in her aunt's London town house while starved of companionship for six lonely years. And now that she was free, both physically and spiritually, she was determined to enjoy every minute of her stay.

Cecilia, too, was enjoying Bath (though she had no interest in reading a boring book about its history). And for the first time since Sophie had come to live with them she realized the felicity of having a close female relation that one could call on at almost any time to accompany one to the shops, or the circulating library, or on a walk through the Royal Crescent at sunset, when the curved row of town houses gleamed gold. So she couldn't account for the times when she resented Sophie's presence. It seemed to happen most frequently when Mr. Hartwell or someone else was congratulating her on possessing such a relation. Cecilia knew Sophie was a treasure (even though she had only belatedly come to that realization), so why would she find it provoking to have others point out such a thing to her?

She surely couldn't be *jealous* of her cousin, could she? It was rather disheartening to find that she could. Though she wasn't sure whether she even wanted Mr. Hartwell for herself, she was very sure she did not want anyone else having him. (Not that there was any danger of Sophie stealing Mr. Hartwell's regard away from her, but Cecilia had noticed Sophie's smiles and was annoyed by them.) And she had also observed at Lucy's wedding banquet that Sir Edmund had sought Sophie out far more frequently than he had her. Cecilia could no longer deceive herself that he did so because he was interested in *her*, as he had never yet invited Cecilia to drive or even asked to call on her, as he had Sophie.

So while Cecilia and Sophie both felt that they had achieved an intimacy that had been lacking in their earlier relationship, they were also conscious of some restraint. They found, though, that by ceasing to speak of Mr. Hartwell or Sir Edmund they were able to maintain cordial relations. And by tacit agreement they both kept Mrs. Foster in the dark about who was enjoying more of Sir Edmund's attentions.

Mrs. Foster, now that the troublesome journey was behind her, was also enjoying herself. She had made an appearance in the Pump Room that morning with the two younger ladies at her side and had discovered some acquaintances from her youth. Most were older married ladies or widows, like herself, who could only offer up boring—and most likely spurious—tales of their various offspring's talents and attractions. Mrs. Foster, however, was able to recount the only slightly exaggerated story of how her niece had engineered the match of the season between Lucy Barrett, a young lady of no more than modest fortune and beauty, and the wealthy and eligible Lord Fitzwalter, while snatching him from under the very nose of the acknowledged toast of the season.

It was probably good that Sophie and Cecilia had left to explore the room together and could not hear this narration, as they would have found it embarrassing, both by its overemphasis of Sophie's talents and its belittling of Lucy's virtues. However, even if the tale was poorly told, it was the most interest that Mrs. Foster had excited in recent memory and, as such, highly satisfying to her. Also satisfying were the accolades she received for her generous acceptance of a "penniless relation" into her home and her gracious treatment of such a one. This assumption by her peers caused no guilt in Mrs. Foster's breast for her prior less than generous treatment of Sophie but did firm her resolve to give no one reason to believe it untrue.

Therefore, Sophie found herself the grateful recipient of various gifts of clothing from her aunt and, even better, much kinder treatment.

So it was that Mrs. Foster, no longer using Sophie as an unpaid chaperone, accompanied both her niece and her daughter to the assembly rooms that evening, determined that her niece would enjoy the gentlemen's attentions as much as any young debutante. Though not quite as much as her own daughter, of course.

If Mr. Hartwell had taken it into his head to kiss his beloved's lips or even her hand that evening, he might have found himself affianced before the end of the night. Cecilia, while not a toast like Priscilla Hammond, was accustomed to having her card full within minutes of arriving in a London ballroom. However, here in Bath she was acquainted with no gentleman but Mr. Hartwell. So at the start of the first set, when Cecilia thought that she was about to have the humiliating experience of sitting out a dance and Mr. Hartwell had suddenly materialized at her side, he had never appeared so prepossessing in her eyes.

While Mr. Hartwell was not aware of the warmer feelings he'd kindled in Cecilia's breast, he was conscious of the fact that she'd never smiled so broadly or meaningfully at him, even seeking his gaze as he handed her off during the course of the dance.

Sophie, observing the two, was happy to see that Cecilia appeared to be appreciating Mr. Hartwell's attentions and hoped it would last. But then she caught a glimpse of someone familiar, and any thoughts of Cecilia and her suitor fled her mind completely.

At first she thought she was imagining it was him. It had been ten years, after all, and he had aged somewhat. Unfortunately, the touch of gray in his sun-streaked hair, which was still the warm shades of autumn leaves, did not detract from his appearance one bit, nor did the small wrinkles at the corners of his very blue eyes. *Though they certainly should,* Sophie thought, annoyed. Something should have rendered him less attractive to her, and if nothing in his appearance did so, at least the memory of how he'd hurt her should make him repellent in her eyes. Unfortunately, her eyes were not cooperating at all. Or perhaps it was her heart? What was it that caused that strange, stirring emotional and physical response to the attributes of some and not others? Why was it that some men who possessed a figure and features that were just as objectively well formed caused not a jolt of feeling, while others, like Sir Edmund and this man, affected her so strongly?

However, he was married now, so there was nothing to worry about, she told herself, calmed by the thought that had once pierced her through. She was surprised she didn't see a woman accompanying him, but no doubt she was nearby. Sophie began looking around for the lady who could be his wife, and so missed his expression when he first saw her. He started with surprise and delight and walked a few paces forward for a closer look. Having satisfied himself as to her identity he moved even closer.

"Sophie!" he said happily as he approached, but then, noticing her aunt Foster's affronted look, amended his greeting. "Miss Lattimore! Fancy meeting you here after all these years." He bowed to her but then looked a little conscious. "I beg your pardon, perhaps it's no longer Miss Lattimore. You are more than likely to have married since we last met . . ." He let the sentence trail off, in an obvious question, and Sophie, having overcome her initial shock and discomfort, smiled coolly at him.

"Good evening, Mr. Maitland. You are correct in addressing me as Miss Lattimore." She hoped he understood that to mean he should *not* be addressing her as Sophie, though it was true she had granted him that liberty ten long years ago. "Aunt Foster, may I introduce Mr. Maitland? Mr. Maitland, my aunt, Mrs. Foster."

Mrs. Foster, confused by Sophie's cold reception of the man as well as his boldness in addressing her niece by her Christian name, gave him a slight nod and even slighter smile. But even she was not proof against his charm.

"It is a pleasure to meet you, Mrs. Foster, though I must beg your pardon for addressing Miss Lattimore with such familiarity. I was accustomed to feeling myself quite one of the family a number of years ago, before my marriage and before Mr. Lattimore's untimely death." Having received a warmer response from Mrs. Foster and an assurance that his apology was accepted, he turned to Sophie. "You must allow me to express my condolences, Miss Lattimore, as belated as they are. I wasn't able to do so at the time, from circumstances beyond my control.

But I am no stranger to that terrible thief, death. You might wonder why you do not see Mrs. Maitland here with me. I am very sorry to say . . ." He paused, apparently overcome by his feelings, and even Sophie's heart could not remain hardened against him in the face of his tragic loss.

"Oh! I am so sorry, Mr. Maitland. When . . . ?"

"It has been a little over a year. I just put off mourning. She left me with two fine children, a boy and a girl."

Sophie did not know what else to say, and there was a short silence before Mr. Maitland's somber expression lightened and he smiled bravely. "But now is not the time to speak of such things. It has been a long time since we danced together, Soph—Miss Lattimore. May I have the honor?"

Sophie was appalled. She'd had no time to assimilate her feelings at seeing Mr. Maitland again so unexpectedly and learning of his wife's death. Mixed with anger and resentment were pity and that fascination she'd always felt for him. The attraction between them was as strong as it had ever been, and she wanted to protect herself, to raise the guards around her heart before interacting too much with him. She scrambled for an excuse.

"I beg your pardon, Mr. Maitland, but I do not dance this evening—" she began, before being interrupted by Mrs. Foster.

"Nonsense, Sophronia, you are not to worry about me or Cecilia." Mrs. Foster turned to Mr. Maitland. "Sophronia is so conscientious of her duty toward her relations.

However, I see an acquaintance of mine, Mrs. Walker," she said, nodding in that lady's direction, "and I will speak to her while you have your dance."

As Sophie still hesitated to place her hand on the one that Mr. Maitland was holding out to her, Mrs. Foster made a little shooing gesture and said, "Go, now. Dance." Sophie felt she had no choice, and tentatively laid her hand on his, touching him as lightly as possible. As soon as she did so he looked ardently into her eyes, as he always used to, and Sophie felt her poor, fragile heart flutter in response.

The set Cecilia had danced with Mr. Hartwell had ended, and she returned to her mother's side just as Sophie took her place on the floor. Sophie could see Cecilia's eyes widen in amazement, but then the music began and Sophie could spare no thought for Cecilia or Aunt Foster, or anyone other than herself and her partner.

It's the dance, she told herself. *You know how you love to dance.* And it was true. She dearly loved to dance, and she'd been missing it all these years. Unfortunately, the person she'd enjoyed dancing with the most was the partner she now had, the man who had humiliated her by his very pointed attentions and then his hasty marriage to another woman. He had captured her heart before breaking it, and she felt that he had to have done so knowingly, such a naïve, unsophisticated young girl she'd been.

"You have not changed at all, you know," he said. "You're still as lovely as you ever were."

"But I *have* changed," Sophie replied, before the steps of the dance took her away from him.

Cecilia watched in shock as Sophie took to the floor with a handsome gentleman she'd never before seen.

"Mama, who is Sophie dancing with?" Cecilia asked as soon as she reached her side. Mrs. Foster had not yet begun a conversation with Mrs. Walker, so only Mr. Hartwell was present.

"A friend of her father's, a Mr. Maitland."

"Are you acquainted with him?" Cecilia asked.

"He was just presented to me. He's a widower with two children."

Cecilia, Mrs. Foster, and Mr. Hartwell turned to watch Sophie and Mr. Maitland as they danced, and Cecilia was heartened to discover that he was older than she'd first thought, probably twice Cecilia's own age, and a widower as well. Actually, quite a good match for Sophie, despite his startling good looks and obvious allure.

Mrs. Foster thought the same, though she at least wanted to inquire as to Mr. Maitland's fortune before consigning her niece to his care. It would be no good at all if he must marry for money, as Sophie had none, but if he was independently situated it was the perfect match for her niece. Mr. Maitland was charming and handsome and seemed to already possess some fondness for Sophie, and as she was practically a spinster, she could not quibble at taking on a few motherless children as part of the bargain. Mrs. Foster was rather proud of herself for tying up her niece's future so neatly. *This talent for matchmaking appears to be a family trait,* she thought with a little chuckle, conveniently forgetting that she and Sophie shared no blood ties, and that she had done nothing to promote the match other than urge a reluctant Sophie to dance.

While the two women watched Sophie and Mr. Maitland, Mr. Hartwell saw a familiar face in the crowd. "By Jove, I do believe it's Sir Edmund," he said, before hailing him.

Greetings had barely been exchanged before Sir Edmund was inquiring after Miss Lattimore, to Cecilia's secret annoyance.

"My niece is dancing with Mr. Maitland," Mrs. Foster announced proudly, nodding in their direction. "They make a handsome couple, wouldn't you agree, Sir Edmund? But my daughter has only been able to dance once thus far, as we have so few acquaintances here in Bath," she said, with all the subtlety of a hatchet.

Sir Edmund perforce offered his arm to Cecilia, requested the honor of a dance, and was promptly accepted.

So it was that Sophie, upon finishing her dance, saw Sir Edmund preparing to dance with Cecilia. She smiled and nodded at him, happier to see him than she'd even anticipated, but either he did not see her or she had overestimated the degree of rapport she thought they had achieved with each other, as he did not respond. Sophie was returned to her aunt by Mr. Maitland and promptly led onto the floor by Mr. Hartwell. She did not see Sir Edmund again after he finished his dance with Cecilia and assumed he must have left the assembly rooms. Their party also left very shortly afterward, as their acquaintance was so slight and Cecilia had danced with all of the gentlemen she knew. They all could not help but feel that Bath had let them down to some degree, after raising their expectations so shamelessly.

5

There was an indisputable grande dame of Bath, a lady whom Mrs. Foster desired to meet more than any other. This was Lady Smallpeace, the Dowager Countess of Ebrington. Lady Smallpeace (who it was said more than lived up to her name) had an unmarried daughter of two-and-thirty, Lady Mary, who lived with her. Lady Smallpeace's son the earl rarely visited Bath, but she was distinguished at present by the visit of her grandnephew, Lord Courtney. The three members of this one household were the most highly ranked of the nobility residing in Bath at present and, almost entirely on this account, were enthusiastically welcomed at every event.

Mrs. Foster, after a quick perusal of *Debrett's Peerage*, was able to trace a tenuous connection to Lady Smallpeace through a second cousin once removed. If Mrs. Foster was unable to achieve an introduction through a mutual acquaintance, she intended to write a letter to Lady Smallpeace informing her of the relationship before calling on her.

It would have surprised Mrs. Foster to know that Lady Smallpeace was also desirous of making *her* family's acquaintance. Lady Smallpeace had heard from another matron the story of Miss Lattimore's matchmaking, and as she had her own very decided opinions on the subject, she was eager to share them with this upstart who appeared to be in need of a set down. (Lady Mary and Lord Courtney were also quite anxious for Lady Smallpeace to meet Miss Lattimore, so that they would not have to listen repeatedly to what she intended to say to her once she did so.)

Lord Courtney had just turned two-and-twenty and was an entirely inoffensive young man. Which is to say he had only a trifling amount of conversation, looks, or charm, but was acknowledged, solely based on his title and material prospects, to be "a very fine gentleman." One of his great-aunt's foremost goals in life was to ensure no undeserving young woman was granted Lord Courtney's attentions. It was presumed by some of the small-minded that she would try to browbeat him into offering for her own (much older) daughter, but such a thought had never occurred to Lady Smallpeace, who had no desire to see her daughter wed. It would serve absolutely no purpose for Lady Smallpeace to lose Lady Mary to another household, as she proved to be a very convenient audience for her mother's many rants; and as for grandchildren, Lady Smallpeace had enough of them to plague her already and could see no profit in having any more.

It was the morning after the assembly that this meeting, greatly desired by all involved, with the exception of Miss Lattimore, finally took place.

Sophie was still reeling from her meeting with Mr. Maitland the evening before and was unable to decide what attitude she should take toward him. She couldn't very well refuse his company after her acceptance of his offer to dance, as to do so now would provoke the very talk she desperately wanted to avoid. She was so confused, her feelings alternating between exhilaration and trepidation, and the one thing she was sure of was that she wanted more time to consider the matter before seeing him again. She greatly feared he intended to pay a call on her that very morning, so when Cecilia and Mrs. Foster expressed a desire to take the waters at the Pump Room, Sophie readily accepted their offer to join them.

Cecilia was very curious about this heretofore unmentioned man in her cousin's life. It was obvious that Mr. Maitland was something more than just a friend of Sophie's father and that he clearly admired Sophie, yet she seemed strangely reticent about him. Mrs. Foster had managed to discover through avid questioning that Mr. Maitland was of independent means and had served in the East India Company in his younger years, where he had made Mr. Lattimore's acquaintance. She had also discovered, through further prodding of a taciturn Sophie, that Maitland's late wife was a woman of fortune. Sophie had not seen Maitland since his betrothal, was unsure where he had settled after his marriage, and had not thought to inquire last night while they were dancing. (Such dilatoriness on her niece's part caused Mrs. Foster to wonder, not for the first time, if her niece's matchmaking ability was highly exaggerated.) Still, Mrs. Foster had learned enough to settle her niece's future for her. Sophie would marry Mr. Maitland and Cecilia would marry Sir Edmund, unless an even more eligible suitor came upon the scene or if Sir Edmund did not come up to scratch.

The more eligible suitor Mrs. Foster had in mind was the viscount currently residing with his great-aunt. While Sir Edmund, as a baronet, ranked higher than a plain Mister Hartwell, a member of the peerage obviously trumped both.

So when Mrs. Walker greeted Mrs. Foster excitedly upon her group's entry into the Pump Room, asking that they accompany her to meet Lady Smallpeace, who had requested the introduction, Mrs. Foster gladly acquiesced, sweeping Cecilia and Sophie along with her.

Not that the girls had any objection to the meeting, as Cecilia, especially, was eager to enlarge her acquaintance. She didn't want a repeat of her first experience at a Bath assembly, where she'd been made to feel practically a wallflower. Sophie, too, was not averse to making new friends, though she soon became aware that once again she should have lowered her expectations.

Lady Mary and Lord Courtney were assessed and almost as quickly dismissed; both of them had such little animation and spoke such inanities when they did open their mouths that Sophie had a difficult time remembering to accord them any attention, and had to force herself to look politely at them when they did venture a sentence or two. As Lady Smallpeace would often speak at exactly the same time, Sophie found this way of conversing very difficult in-deed, and wondered if the countess was so accustomed to ignoring her daughter and grandnephew that she wasn't even aware they were talking. Because of their manner of conversing it took Sophie a few minutes to realize that *she* was the subject under discussion, though it could not really be termed a discussion but more of a diatribe. And Lady Mary's jovial reaction to her mother's speech was so oppo-site of what one might expect that Sophie continued to wonder for a few minutes if she were being reprimanded or praised.

"Miss Lattimore," said Lady Smallpeace loudly, "your circumstances in life are such that I am amazed you took it upon yourself to meddle in the parental rights of those of a much higher situation."

Halfway through this sentence, while her mother was still speaking, Lady Mary tittered and said: "Such a pretty spencer Miss Lattimore is wearing. The trimming, espe-cially, is so very nice. Don't you agree, Miss Foster? But Miss Foster, your spencer is very attractive, too. What a lovely shade of blue! Probably London-made, and yours, too, Miss Lattimore. Yours is just as pretty as Miss Foster's, though not the same style, of course. Not the same style or color, but both *very* attractive."

In the middle of her daughter's discourse on the young ladies' jackets, Lady Smallpeace launched into another ringing criticism of Sophie's audacity in interfering with the marital prospects of a gentleman of Lord Fitzwalter's standing, interrupting herself to ask Sophie: "And your parents, Miss Lattimore? Who exactly are they? Deceased, both of them, I've heard."

Lady Smallpeace made this seem like a grave fault on Sophie's part, and Sophie wondered if she had never been taught that you ought to express *condolences*, not condemnation, when one had lost one's relatives.

But this was the opening Mrs. Foster, undaunted by Lady Smallpeace's unfriendly demeanor, had been waiting for. "Actually, Lady Smallpeace, our families are distantly connected. My husband's grandmother's sister was Lady Vickery, née Miss Amelia Fortescue, whose granddaughter, Miss Elizabeth Brandon, married—"

"My second cousin, Lord Tidmarsh, Marquis of Mount Edgecombe!" Lady Smallpeace finished triumphantly. After making this pronouncement her face shifted into some kind of strange contortion that Sophie and the Foster ladies were finally able to determine (after some consideration) was an expression of pleasure, though none would go so far as to describe it as a smile.

It was at this point that Lady Smallpeace actually took notice of Cecilia, who was looking especially pretty in a color that Lady Mary had already mentioned was very flattering. "You're to be congratulated on your daughter, Mrs. Foster," Lady Smallpeace said, as she stared at Cecilia. "She seems to be a very modest young woman." This remark was punctuated with a glance of disapproval at Sophie, as if to make obvious the contrast between the cousins. However, Lady Smallpeace's glare was only half as scathing as the ones she'd been directing at Sophie before she'd learned of the connection between their families.

"Sit here, Mrs. Foster, beside me. I would learn more of your relations. The young people will go take the waters." Lady Smallpeace turned to her daughter. "Make sure your cousin takes his, Mary. I've seen him pouring it out when he thinks I'm not looking." Then, when Lord Courtney scoffed at such an accusation and protested that he was in perfect health and not in need of such a cure, Lady Smallpeace said: "Nonsense! It is especially beneficial for a young man in the prime of life. It fortifies the blood and strengthens your masculine vitality."

No one knew what Lady Smallpeace was referencing when she mentioned Lord Courtney's "masculine vitality," but they all felt that it was probably something that should not be discussed in public. (Sophie actually feared she meant to say "virility" but got the words confused.) So the young people were quick to obey the dowager countess' command to go, and leave her and Mrs. Foster to their discussion. As they left they could hear Lady Smallpeace asking: "The Fosters are a Northumberland family, I believe? Established there before the Battle of Hastings, were they not?"

Lord Courtney gave his arm to Cecilia, who accepted it with a coquettish look, and Sophie fell into step beside Lady Mary. Before Sophie could venture on to a topic of conversation, Lady Mary began speaking endlessly without pausing for a reply, leaving Sophie with little to do other than suppress the yawn she could feel building inside her.

But then Sophie chided herself for being ungenerous. Lady Mary was probably conscious of her mother's rudeness and only sought to divert attention from it. It had to be very difficult to be the daughter of such a woman. So Sophie redoubled her efforts to pay attention to her companion's speech, which was now centered on the difficulty of finding reliable chairmen to transport her mother's custom-designed sedan chair. Sophie had to concentrate very intensely, as Lady Mary had a soft voice, and by this time of day the crowds had greatly increased, as had their volume, and the band was diligently doing its best to compete with them, the trumpet player in particular. Sophie hoped that the famous waters had properties that would alleviate any headache she had by the time she reached them.

They finally made it to the pump, and as they waited for the attendant to hand them a glass of water Sophie became conscious of someone's eyes upon her. Looking around, she saw Sir Edmund barely ten feet away, and her face lit up in response.

Sir Edmund was frowning slightly, but when he saw her pleased reaction, his expression cleared and he came forward, bowing to her. He bowed to Lady Mary as well, who smiled and murmured a greeting, but as the attendant handed Lady Mary her glass of water almost immediately after this interaction, there was no opportunity for further speech. While Lady Mary was distracted, Sophie seized the opportunity to step away from her and closer to Sir Edmund. As Sophie's place was immediately taken by an acquaintance of Lady Mary, who began speaking with her, Sophie congratulated herself that she would not even be missed.

She wondered if Sir Edmund thought she hadn't *wished* to speak to him at the assembly the previous evening; his expression when he had seen her there seemed much cooler than usual (and she was sure, after much reflection during a wakeful night, that he *had* seen her) and her disappointment at giving him a mistaken impression was almost as great as her agitation at seeing Mr. Maitland again after so many years. So she was determined to make Sir Edmund understand she remained his friend. If that, indeed, was what he intended her to be.

"Sir Edmund! I saw you at the assembly last night but I had no opportunity to speak to you—"

"Yes, you were engaged at the time. In a dance, I mean," he said, a little jerkily. He seemed as nervous and uncomfortable as she.

"Oh, yes. I was. Mr. Maitland is an old—that is, he was a friend of my father's. From my youth."

"Your youth, Miss Lattimore?" he asked, his expression relaxing a little. "Perhaps you mean your childhood. You are obviously still in your youth."

He used this as an excuse to examine her face closely, and she lowered her eyes to avoid looking into his own, as she found it difficult to think when she did so. "I am eight-and-twenty," she said, as if contradicting his assumption that she was young, though she could not understand why she did so. She wondered, not for the first time, why she automatically thwarted any flirtatious overtures. It was almost as if she didn't feel she was worthy of such attention.

"Elderly, indeed. Just two years younger than my advanced age," he said, and she was pleased to finally learn how old he was.

"Perhaps we should both drink the water," Sophie suggested playfully. "It is reputed to be a fountain of youth."

They had been walking as they talked and had wandered a good distance away from the pump, a realization Sir Edmund came to after Sophie's comment. "My apologies, Miss Lattimore, I prevented you from taking the waters and have separated you from your companions. Shall I return you to them?"

He began peering over the crowd, and Sophie assumed he was searching for Lady Mary or the Fosters.

"Oh, no! Please, I'd much rather remain with you," she said, far more enthusiastically than was perhaps wise. She could feel her cheeks growing warm, and hurriedly changed the subject. "Are you to stay in Bath, Sir Edmund? Or are you here for a short visit?"

"My plans are not fixed as of yet," he said, in a tone and with a glance at her that suggested she might have a bearing on them. Or so she hoped. But then she recalled his purpose in being there was to meet prospective brides and told herself yet again that she must view him as a friend and nothing more.

"Have you been able to widen your circle of female acquaintances since coming to Bath?" Sophie asked.

"I was introduced to Lady Smallpeace and Lady Mary and danced with Miss Foster. You were engaged, if you recall."

"But you are already acquainted with me and my cousin. You are supposed to look about you for other eligible ladies."

"If you are finally offering to act as a matchmaker for me, I believe it is your job to find the lady," Sir Edmund said, but he was obviously joking.

"I see you will never bring the thing off if left to your own devices. I may have no choice but to take a hand in the matter." Sophie briefly scanned the room and saw a group of young ladies peering interestedly in Sir Edmund's direction while whispering behind their fans and giggling. "I think a mature lady would be a better choice, not a girl who has only just left the schoolroom and put up her hair. Do you have any objection to a widow?" Sophie asked.

"Such as Lady Smallpeace, perchance?"

Sophie laughed. "I am not certain she would entertain your suit, Sir Edmund. No, it should be someone who is neither a child nor a sixty-year-old dowager."

"In other words, someone about your age," he said, and Sophie looked suspiciously at him, wondering if she was meant to read anything into his remark. His face gave nothing away, however, and before she could respond she heard her name being called.

Sophie turned to find Mr. Maitland approaching, a warm expression on his face. "Miss Lattimore, how delightful to see you again."

"Good morning, Mr. Maitland," Sophie said, before turning to Sir Edmund, who was standing stiffly by her side. "Sir Edmund, may I present Mr. Maitland?"

The two gentlemen nodded at each other, Mr. Maitland smiling broadly, Sir Edmund's expression much more restrained.

"I believe we have met before, have we not, Sir Edmund?" Mr. Maitland asked.

"Possibly, though I am sorry to say I do not recall the occasion."

"Perhaps it is my memory that is at fault," Mr. Maitland said, as cordial as ever.

The three stood in silence for a moment, a silence that seemed fraught with tension, before Sir Edmund spoke. "If you will excuse us, Mr. Maitland, I was just about to escort Miss Lattimore to the pump."

"But I was headed that way as well! I rarely go a day without partaking of the waters. So very salubrious," Mr. Maitland said. "Shall we go together?"

Mr. Maitland held out his arm to Sophie, and with a glance at Sir Edmund, she put her hand on Mr. Maitland's arm, feeling she had no other choice. She wondered if Sir Edmund would offer his arm as well, but it seemed she was not to enjoy the distinction of having the two handsomest men in the room on each arm. Sir Edmund merely bowed and said, "Since you already have an escort, Miss Lattimore, I beg you to excuse me. Good day."

Sophie was disappointed at Sir Edmund's departure, but found she was not given much time to regret his absence, as Mr. Maitland was particularly talkative and charming and seemed determined to keep her well entertained.

Cecilia was not finding her escort nearly as entertaining. They had reached the pump long before Sophie, where Lord Courtney had gallantly retrieved a glass for Cecilia but refused to drink any himself.

"Don't tell my aunt, but I loathe the stuff. Tastes like it's been warming in a puddle by the side of the road."

Since he said this just as Cecilia had taken her first sip, she suddenly found it very difficult to swallow and wished he'd kept his observations to himself. But she was also conscious of the fact that Lord Courtney was the wealthiest, highest-ranking gentleman in the room, and that other young ladies were casting envious glances her way. Even without her mother's explicit instructions, Cecilia recognized that Lord Courtney was the preeminent matrimonial prize of her generation and that it behooved her to make the most of this opportunity.

But he certainly wasn't making it easy for her.

"I wonder if it's the pigs that cause the funny smell," he mused aloud.

"The pigs?" Cecilia echoed.

"You must have heard; some diseased nobleman's swine nosed out the springs. In the last century. May have been King George's pigs. Daresay inhaling too much of the odor is what led to his mental, uh, incapacitation," Lord Courtney said, tapping the side of his forehead with his finger. "By Jove, I should tell my great-aunt so. So much for masculine vitality, what?" he asked, laughing aloud at his genius in disproving Lady Smallpeace's claim.

Cecilia was not, by any stretch of the imagination, an intellectual, but even she recognized that Lord Courtney's statement was erroneous. She remembered a story about a leprous prince and his pigs but, though she had only the foggiest knowledge of the history of the Britons, knew that the discovery had occurred a thousand years ago at least, and probably more than two thousand. It definitely had not occurred during the life span of their current mad king. And when Lord Courtney pointed to the statue of Beau Nash that hovered in a niche above them and said: "That's King George there. Has a look of the prince regent about him, doesn't he?" it was all Cecilia could do not to spit her water in his face.

So when Mr. Hartwell turned up at that very moment, he once again had the appearance of a savior in her eyes. Cecilia immediately presented him to Lord Courtney, pleased to have an excuse to change the subject before she lost her composure completely.

The two gentlemen exchanged pleasantries and Cecilia was able to bring herself under control. But seeing the two men side by side, Cecilia realized that she had been wont to grossly undervalue Mr. Hartwell's attractions. Certainly he was not as darkly handsome as Sir Edmund, nor quite as tall, but he had a vigorous, healthy appearance, and he was more muscular than Lord Courtney, who, if not a viscount, would have been rightly labeled a spindle-shanks.

But then Cecilia immediately chided herself for even noticing the gentlemen's legs. Firstly, it was vastly improper, and secondly, it had absolutely no bearing on the very serious business of choosing a husband.

6

$\mathcal{S}$ophie and Mr. Maitland, having drunk their water with only minimal grimacing, were making their way across the room to Mrs. Foster when Mr. Maitland stopped in the middle of a sentence, his attention arrested by something or someone. Sophie, following the direction of his gaze, was surprised to see Priscilla Beswick, née Hammond, enter the room.

"What a handsome creature," Mr. Maitland murmured, and Sophie cast him a look of annoyance.

"I can introduce you, if you'd like," Sophie said.

It occurred to Mr. Maitland that Sophie was somewhat affronted. "What interest do I have in other ladies when you are here, Sophie?" he said huskily, treating her to one of those smoldering glances he'd perfected.

"That is an intriguing question," Sophie replied. "One that I've wondered myself."

Mr. Maitland was momentarily bereft of speech, and Sophie was glad of it. She'd noticed he'd fallen back into the habit of using her Christian name, and this tendency and his seductive tone had again roused her defenses. If a different gentleman had commented on the appearance of another woman in her presence, it would not have bothered her; she knew she could not compete with Priscilla Beswick's physical attractions and was not jealous of her incredible beauty. It would be dishonest if a man pretended *not* to notice. But when Mr. Maitland praised Priscilla, and so ardently, it could only remind Sophie of his past betrayal and make her wonder if he had really changed. Was he again playing some cruel game with her?

While this exchange was occurring, Priscilla had seen Sophie and had immediately approached her. "Miss Lattimore," she said, inclining her head.

"Mrs. Beswick, how do you do?" Sophie asked, and upon hearing she was well, introduced Mr. Maitland.

"Your devoted servant, Mrs. Beswick," Maitland said, and Sophie restrained herself from rolling her eyes. It was a harmless platitude, it was true, but he didn't have to say it quite so enthusiastically.

Priscilla was evidently as impressed by Mr. Maitland as he was by her and flashed him a brilliant smile.

"Is Mr. Beswick in Bath with you?" Sophie said, as she thought Priscilla might need to be reminded she was already married.

"Charles?" Priscilla asked, as if there were a different Mr. Beswick Sophie might be referring to. "No, he is not with me. He is at home, in Devon. He rarely travels. He vastly prefers the country over town," she said in a puzzled tone, as if it were an incomprehensible preference.

"If he is a man of good sense, then he'd surely prefer to be wherever his charming lady is," Maitland said, and Sophie did roll her eyes, just a little, but was confident the other two would not notice. And they did not, as they were fully occupied in looking at each other. Sophie had to admit they made an engaging tableau, as they were two of the handsomest representations of their sex she'd ever seen and watching them together was like viewing the subjects of a Boucher or Fragonard painting brought to life.

"It is good to see you, Mrs. Beswick, but it appears as if my party is preparing to go," Sophie said, nodding toward where Mrs. Foster and Cecilia stood waiting. "I must take my leave of you. I hope to see you again while you're in Bath."

"But, Miss Lattimore, I insist upon us meeting again, so you need not hope in vain," Priscilla said. "I will call on you. Where are you staying?"

Sophie gave her the address, and Priscilla replied that she had taken lodgings very near to Sophie on Catharine Place, by which time, Mrs. Foster and Cecilia had joined them. Mrs. Foster had to be introduced to Priscilla Beswick, but Cecilia was well acquainted with her, though this was their first meeting since Lord Fitzwalter had wed Cecilia's friend Lucy instead of Priscilla, and so Cecilia was a trifle ill at ease. But Priscilla laughed and joked and complimented Cecilia as if they'd been bosom friends of many years' standing instead of just casual acquaintances.

After they left the Pump Room and were waiting for a chair for Mrs. Foster, Cecilia turned to Sophie in wonder. "Why do you think Priscilla Beswick has come to Bath? It's most peculiar, her being so newly married. And she traveled here on her own, without her husband. What do you make of it?"

But Sophie did not know *what* to make of it. She only knew it appeared Priscilla Beswick may not be entirely happy with her marriage. And that she might feel Sophie was to blame.

After the ladies had returned to their lodgings, Mrs. Foster had much to say about the morning's activities.

"Cecilia, I was very pleased with your appearance and demeanor this morning. It was obvious Lord Courtney was similarly delighted."

"Lord Courtney," Sophie said, surprised. "Surely you do not think of *him* for Cecilia."

Mrs. Foster smiled benignly at her niece. "I understand, Sophronia, where you would think it somewhat . . . ambitious of me to encourage Cecilia to look so high, but in this case I do not think it matters that her dowry is no larger. Lady Smallpeace assured me that family background is her foremost consideration when seeking a bride for her grandnephew, and now that she is aware of our family connection, coupled with Cecilia's modest and ladylike demeanor, I do think she'd consider her a suitable wife for Lord Courtney."

"But . . . what do family background and fortune matter if there are no tender feelings? Cecilia, you cannot tell me you are interested in Lord Courtney?"

Before Cecilia could answer, Mrs. Foster did. "Sophronia! I am beginning to believe the recent popularity you've experienced has gone to your head, just as Lady Smallpeace prophesied! It is true that your intervention on Lord Fitzwalter's behalf was a propitious one; Priscilla Hammond had nothing but her beauty to recommend her and was obviously an unwise choice for a gentleman of Lord Fitzwalter's standing. But in general, such matters should be left to older and wiser family members. A match should not be entered into based solely, or even primarily, upon sentiment, which can fade over time. If Cecilia marries Lord Courtney, her son will be a viscount!"

Sophie desperately wanted to retort: "And an idiot," but felt that might anger her aunt even further. And it was true that, while Lord Fitzwalter and Lucy seemed to be happy, Sophie's interference in Priscilla and Charles Beswick's affairs did not seem to have worked out as well for them, so she could certainly not claim to be an expert in these matters. Also, Sophie saw no point in borrowing trouble; it was early days yet and Lord Courtney might not come up to scratch. In which case Cecilia would most likely seriously consider the suit of Mr. Hartwell, who Sophie persisted in thinking was a far better match for her cousin. So she decided to hold her tongue for the present, though she very much disagreed with her aunt's sentiments.

However, Mrs. Foster wasn't yet finished. "While we are on this subject, Sophronia, I also wanted to congratulate *you* on having attached Mr. Maitland."

"Congratulate me on . . . what?"

"I do realize he hasn't yet formally requested your hand, but it is fairly obvious he means to court you in earnest, and I know your dear parents would have been pleased to see you settled so well."

"And he's so handsome, cousin! Not that that's important, of course," Cecilia finished a trifle disconsolately, remembering that her new beau was nothing to brag about in that regard.

"Handsome is as handsome does," Mrs. Foster pronounced, though Sophie did not understand how this was pertinent to the discussion at hand.

"I am not on the verge of an engagement, Aunt Foster. I do not know why you should believe that I am."

"Why, if you are not, then I find your behavior rather fast, to say the least. I was forced to give Lady Smallpeace an inkling of the matter when she wondered who it was that you were walking with."

"Aunt Foster, I wish you would not spread gossip about me and Mr. Maitland, or indeed, about me and any other gentleman. I have no knowledge of Mr. Maitland's intentions, and it is not the thing to be bragging about a conquest before it is made!"

This was too much for Mrs. Foster, who had never heard

any criticism from her niece and was highly affronted that Sophie dared to offer it now. "Who are you, young lady, to counsel me on appropriate behavior? I think you have forgotten your place in this household. Perhaps you should go to your room and meditate upon it."

Sophie stifled any reply she desired to make, stood up regally, and marched from the room. As she passed Cecilia she saw how very distressed her young cousin was. But Sophie could not bring herself to smile reassuringly at her, she was so upset herself.

An hour or so later Cecilia knocked on the door of Sophie's chamber before slipping inside. She found her cousin lying on the bed, though she was not sleeping. Cecilia sat down on the edge of the bed beside her.

"Sophie, I am so sorry, but I know my mother meant it for the best. She and I both believed you and Mr. Maitland to have an understanding, he looks at you so warmly. Indeed, he appears to have worn the willow for you for many years."

"While he was married to another woman and she was bearing his children?" Sophie asked sarcastically.

Cecilia flushed and looked away. "I admit I do not quite understand. He appears to have a regard for you, but as you said, he did marry elsewhere. Were you too young when he knew you before?"

Sophie sighed and sat up in bed. "No, it is I who must apologize. If I had explained my history with Mr. Maitland, perhaps my aunt would not have assumed what she did. But really, I do not understand him clearly myself."

Sophie paused, and Cecilia waited without speaking for her to continue, even when the silence seemed to stretch on a little too long. Cecilia was beginning to realize there was something painful about her cousin's past dealings with Mr. Maitland, and she did not want to distress her any further by saying something she ought not.

"I was your age; I had just turned eighteen, when he came to visit my father, whom he had met when they both worked for the East India Company. I had recently come out and I was moderately popular. Of course, I didn't have a grand London debut like you, but at local assemblies and private balls my dance card was always full, and there was one young man in particular. He wasn't dashing or romantic, but we were friends and there was the possibility of something more . . . when Mr. Maitland showed up.

"And Mr. Maitland *was* dashing and romantic, so I quickly forgot about this other young man and spent all of my time with him instead. Rides in his curricle, supper dances; we paired off whenever possible and flirted enthusiastically with each other, while managing to stay within the bounds of propriety. It was very obvious he was courting me, and the neighborhood considered it just a matter of time before our engagement was announced. As did I."

Sophie smiled self-deprecatingly. "Instead of announcing his engagement to me, he left the neighborhood altogether before announcing his betrothal to another young woman. I only heard of it through a mutual acquaintance;

he hadn't the decency to tell me himself. My father wanted to go after him and take him to task, but I begged him to let it rest, as I felt it would only stir up more talk if he were to pursue Mr. Maitland. And I was worried, too, that it might result in a duel, and Papa would get injured or even killed. How could I live with myself if my silly folly, fancying Mr. Maitland was in love with me, resulted in another person's injury or death? It was not worth it. But I found that whatever popularity I'd enjoyed before Mr. Maitland's arrival completely dissipated at his departure. It was widely rumored that I'd jilted him, and my behavior, which would have been perfectly acceptable if our engagement had been announced, was considered fast indeed when undertaken with a man betrothed to a different lady.

"The invitations dried up, and no one asked me to dance at the few assemblies I did attend. It was less painful to stop going out, especially once my father's health began to deteriorate. So I became what you see: a spinster content to sit in the shadows, her one grand love tainted by scandal."

Cecilia sat for a moment more in silence, stunned by what she'd heard. "Cousin, I wonder that you did not slap his face or give him the cut direct upon seeing him again."

Sophie smiled. "I wonder the same. I was so taken aback, and then he was asking me to dance like nothing had happened, and I did *not* want to stir up that old gossip." She shrugged. "And I still cannot help wondering if there is some explanation that would excuse him, and I am very eager to hear it. Especially since I have been accustomed to thinking of him as my lost love these past ten years."

"I'm not sure *anything* could excuse him," Cecilia said, and Sophie remembered what it was like to be eighteen and feel such righteous indignation.

"It is not entirely his fault. He's probably not even aware of how I was treated after he left. And it's very easy to see things from one's own point of view. Perhaps he thought it no more than a trifling flirtation and doesn't feel he wronged me at all."

"But to lead you on in such a manner—"

"Yes, that is what I cannot entirely excuse. Perhaps I imagined his feelings for me, but he had to have known I believed myself in love with him. I was too unsophisticated to hide it. And I was only eighteen, while he was six-and-twenty. Certainly old enough to recognize he'd turned a silly young girl's head."

"And are you still in love with him?" Cecilia asked.

Sophie considered for a moment. "I do not know what it is I feel, exactly, but there is still *something* significant between us. I don't understand what it is, I can't put a name to it, only that it's as if I feel a sort of . . . *ache* when he is near me. And I am scared that he will break my heart again."

"But . . . what if he does want to marry you this time?"

Sophie got up from the bed and walked to the window. It had begun to rain, a quick afternoon storm, but the sun was somehow still shining. A sunshower. If she were superstitious perhaps she could read something into it, but

she was not, and she had enough difficulties trying to figure out her life as it was, without throwing weather phe-
nomena into the mix. "I do not know," Sophie said, just
when Cecilia was beginning to think she was not going to
answer her question. "I wish I could say I would refuse
him, but I just don't know. He would be offering me all the
things I've missed out on: marriage, children, a home." Sophie turned back to face Cecilia. "I do not mean to complain; your mother was kind to take me in, and I'm truly,
truly grateful. But it's a precarious and insecure existence
being dependent on others for the very roof over one's
head, and while I have a place to live, I don't feel as if I
have a *home*. And as a single woman of no fortune I have
very little prospect of ever having one of my own. Marriage would give me that, at least."

Cecilia felt as if she were seeing her cousin for the first
time. To think that Sophie had lived with them for six
years and Cecilia had never known she felt this way. She
jumped up from the bed and ran to hug her. "Cousin, I am
so sorry. I promise you that things will change. We *are*
your family and you *do* have a home with us."

They were both crying a little, and smiling, too, and
Sophie felt as if *she* were a sunshower. When she'd gathered her composure, she said: "Cecilia, your case is totally
different from mine, but you can still benefit from my
mistakes. Please do not feel as if you have to rush into anything. If I hadn't been so quick to imagine myself in love
with Mr. Maitland, I would have not opened myself up to
such disappointment and humiliation. You have financial

security and a happy home. You do not *need* to marry, and you can certainly take your time deciding if and whom you will marry."

Cecilia nodded but wouldn't quite meet her cousin's eyes, and Sophie realized she probably did not want to accept advice from an impoverished spinster who had just announced she lived a fruitless existence.

"What will you do about Mr. Maitland?" Cecilia asked.

"I will be much more circumspect than I was the first time. It was very distressing to hear your mother saying some of the same things that were said of me ten years ago, and I refuse to open myself up to censure again. I will make it very plain to him that I will not be trifled with."

But Sophie found those words easier to say than to act upon. Mr. Maitland was once again everywhere she was, and she found it difficult to strike a balance between showing disinterested friendliness and encouraging his suit. He appeared to be courting her even more assiduously than he had the first time, and it did feel as if he was sincere in his affection for her. Sophie began to believe he *had* loved her ten years ago but had been tempted by his deceased wife's fortune into making a much more advantageous marriage. Perhaps the wise thing would be to do as Cecilia advised and cut his acquaintance completely, but a part of her was still tempted. She had loved him once and had desired above all things to be his wife, and here she was being given a second chance. Would it not be foolish of her to throw away such an opportunity and return to her prior empty existence as a poor relation?

Though it was true that her situation in her aunt's home had improved and continued to do so. Cecilia had spoken with her mother, and while Mrs. Foster would never be truly affectionate toward Sophie—it was just not in her nature—Sophie's story had stirred her aunt's compassion. If Mrs. Foster understood nothing else, she understood how a lady's entire future was tied up in her ability to marry and marry well. And it was no secret that a gentleman could toy with a young woman's affections, ruin *her* reputation, and suffer no ill effects of his own. So while Mrs. Foster would never deign to apologize to her niece, she did refrain from any more discussion of her niece's suitor, in public or private.

Sophie eventually decided her best course of action would be to follow the advice she herself had given Sir Edmund when he'd asked how he could get to know a young lady without raising unfulfilled expectations. Sophie decided that she would not pair off with Mr. Maitland like she had when she was young and foolish, but instead only spend time with him when in the company of others. She was aided in this endeavor by an unexpected ally: Mrs. Priscilla Beswick.

Mrs. Beswick seemed to pop up whenever Sophie and Mr. Maitland were together, and though Mr. Maitland refrained from giving her as much attention as he did Sophie, Priscilla certainly appeared to delight in the attention he did give her. Sophie was eventually forced to conclude that Priscilla, who had gloried in being the Toast of the Town, was not content to give up that title in exchange for that of "Mrs. Beswick."

Sophie was not given long to wonder why Priscilla Beswick had come to Bath, for she soon paid her promised call on Sophie, finding her at home alone. Cecilia and Mrs. Foster had gone to the Pump Room to meet Lady Smallpeace, Lord Courtney, and Lady Mary, but Sophie had decided she'd had enough of the Noble Nitwits (as she referred to them in her thoughts) and preferred to stay home and read.

She reluctantly put her book away when Priscilla was announced and got up from her seat to shake hands with her before inviting her to sit and offering her some refreshments.

Once the servant had left the room, Priscilla turned to Sophie, a serious expression on her face. "I must admit, Miss Lattimore, I came on purpose because I wanted to speak to you in private. When I did not see you in the Pump Room with the Fosters, I hoped I might find you alone."

Sophie found this pronouncement somewhat alarming. She could not think of any reason Priscilla Beswick might desire to speak with her privately, other than to berate her for interfering in her affairs. So she just smiled as encouragingly as she was able and hoped it was not to be a long visit.

"You must wonder why I desired to speak with you, but I beg you to answer my questions before I answer yours. How did you know, as you wrote in your letter to

Lord Fitzwalter, that I had an attachment to a different gentleman? Do you have occult powers, perhaps? Because not even our most intimate of friends were privy to our secret."

Sophie realized she should have expected this question. It must truly be a mystery to Priscilla how someone she was barely acquainted with could have known about her personal affairs. "I must apologize, Mrs. Beswick. It probably seems a horrible invasion of privacy that I discovered your secret. It was unintentional, I assure you, and I told no one other than Lord Fitzwalter. And even then, I did not tell him the name of the gentleman—"

"I do realize that, Miss Lattimore. Lord Fitzwalter read me the letter. Or, at least, he read me the portion that applied to me." Priscilla got up from her seat and began to pace the room. "He was very kind. He mentioned that he would accept my word over that of an anonymous letter-writer. But I found that when he asked me directly if I had already given my heart to someone, I could not lie to him." Priscilla grimaced. "Though I later wondered if I should have."

Sophie began an incoherent apology, but Priscilla motioned her to silence. "You need not apologize. I must admit I was angered by your interference, but I was able to forgive you when I recognized it to be my Christian duty to do so." Sophie couldn't help feeling this was not the most comprehensive of absolutions. "But I must know," Priscilla continued, "how did you discover the truth about me and Charles? It is driving me mad not knowing. When Lord Fitzwalter first approached me he did not know who authored the letter, either, so I thought I was doomed to live in ignorance. But then a London friend wrote to me and told me that you had done it and I just had to know how you found out."

Sophie was embarrassed to have to confess and wished she could think of some way to paint her behavior in a more glamorous light. "I was an unseen witness to an episode between you and Mr. Beswick at a ball. I had gone out onto a balcony for some fresh air, and you also came out and launched into speech before I could make my presence known. And then you disappeared just as quickly."

"Oh, dear," Priscilla said, turning red in embarrassment. "I know which incident you refer to; Charles only attended one ball during my London season, but I cannot remember exactly what words we exchanged. I guess I should count myself fortunate that you did not repeat the conversation to anyone."

"Of course I would never do that! And I would not have taken it upon myself to write that letter had I not been aware of Miss Barrett's partiality for Lord Fitzwalter, and that your attachment to him did not appear to be as strong. Though perhaps I was mistaken?" Sophie asked, as she realized, from her own experience, that public observation was not always the best indicator of personal feelings, and she was starting to regret having involved herself in the entire affair.

"No, you were correct in your assumption that my feelings for Charles were stronger than my feelings for Lord Fitzwalter. But"—and Priscilla quickly crossed the room to throw herself on the sofa next to Sophie and grab her hands—"Miss Lattimore, mightn't I have been mistaken in my feelings? I thought it was an answer to a prayer, that letter, allowing me to honestly admit my attachment and follow my heart, but what if my heart was mistaken? What if my greatest happiness did not lie with Charles, as I thought, but with Lord Fitzwalter?" Her voice dropped to a whisper. "I may have destroyed any future happiness I once thought to possess."

And then tears welled up in those crystalline green eyes that were staring so soulfully and mournfully at Sophie.

Sophie felt that this might possibly be the most awkward and uncomfortable moment she had ever experienced. Her hands, growing damp with perspiration, were clutched in Priscilla Beswick's, who sat far too close, peering into Sophie's eyes as if in search of answers that Sophie knew she did not possess. And yet she felt she could not be the first to move away, as Priscilla could very well interpret that as a rejection of her and the confidences she was sharing. So Sophie spent an interminable length of time in exquisite discomfort, in such enforced proximity that she could smell the kippers Priscilla had apparently eaten for breakfast, and wondered that Priscilla did not feel uncomfortable herself. Finally, at long last, Priscilla drew back, and Sophie took the opportunity to inch away even further while Priscilla was busy wiping her eyes dry with her handkerchief.

"I beg your pardon, Miss Lattimore," Priscilla said, having composed herself. "I did not mean to give vent to my emotions as I did."

Sophie wished fervently that she had not but was beginning to wonder if Priscilla enjoyed enacting dramatic scenes. Sophie thought it strange that such a beautiful young woman felt so starved for attention that she must seek it out at every opportunity, but this appeared to be the case. Still, Priscilla seemed genuinely distressed, and Sophie reflected that she had no choice but to try to assist her, as it was entirely her own fault for involving herself in Priscilla's affairs in the first place.

Priscilla proceeded to explain to Sophie that she and Charles Beswick had known each other all of their lives, but it wasn't until Charles had returned home from school and seen Priscilla (nearly) all grown up that things took a turn for the romantic. But it appeared that Charles' idea of romance did not match that of Priscilla's, as she told Sophie in comprehensive detail.

"I had a brand-new trousseau made by Madame Devy on Bond Street. You are aware, Miss Lattimore, of how exquisite her designs are! Why, Mama had to sulk for nearly a week to get my father to agree to commission her. He felt that the clothes I'd had made for my come-out were sufficient. Men! But I've wandered from the point. The point is, I've had no occasion to wear any of my new trousseau since our wedding! At least, not until I came here, to Bath." She paused to smooth the skirt of her very smart walking dress lovingly before looking inquiringly at Sophie.

"Beautiful. Very chic," Sophie murmured, and this seemed to satisfy Priscilla, for she resumed her story.

"Charles' idea of a honeymoon was to go to his brother's hunting lodge; a dreary, dismal, poky little house in the middle of nowhere with absolutely no society."

"Perhaps he wanted to spend time with you alone," Sophie suggested.

"If that is true, he did not say so. He rarely ever compliments me, Miss Lattimore. I might as well be a dried-up old spinster for all the sweet words I have from him. I do beg your pardon," she interrupted herself to say to Sophie, who could only infer Priscilla thought she was offended by the words "dried-up old spinster," which Sophie had not been until Priscilla apologized for saying them. Before Sophie could respond Priscilla continued: "Lord Fitzwalter always noticed whenever I wore a new dress and would even mention the effect wearing a certain color had upon my complexion."

"But Mrs. Beswick, you cannot expect marriage to be a constant stream of compliments on your appearance!" Priscilla did not appear to agree with this statement and merely blinked in response. Sophie decided a change of tactics was in order. "What caused you to fall in love with Mr. Beswick in the first place? What did you talk about when you were courting?"

Priscilla sighed, and her face took on a dreamy expression. Sophie was a little encouraged, feeling this was a positive sign. "He told me that while he was away at school it was like an awkward calf had transformed into a prize South Devon heifer. Because of my hair, you understand," Priscilla said modestly. And though Sophie realized that the South Devon breed was famous for its copper color and Priscilla's hair was a similar shade of light reddish-brown, she wondered that Priscilla was lamenting the lack of compliments such as these.

But Sophie was not about to point out any of Charles' defects as a suitor. There had to be something that had brought these two together; something that a future relationship could be based upon.

Something other than Priscilla's resemblance to Charles' favorite type of cow.

7

ophie had not forgotten the other duty she had reluctantly agreed to assume, that of finding Sir Edmund a potential bride. She did not know which task was more onerous; assisting Priscilla with her marriage or assisting Sir Edmund *into* one. But Sophie wished to keep Sir Edmund as a friend, and she very much understood his dilemma and appreciated his sensitivity in not wanting to do to another lady what Sophie had had done to her. So over the next few weeks she began looking in earnest for a likely match for him.

While doing so she noticed Cecilia eyeing him with interest again. Torn between a brilliant match with the colorless Lord Courtney or the less wealthy and high-ranking but much more attractive Sir Edmund, Cecilia had obviously started reassessing her options. But Sophie really did not feel Sir Edmund and Cecilia would suit and, what is more, she did not think he himself saw Cecilia as a potential bride. He paid her no special attention, only according her the same polite courtesy as he did her mother. He did not even look at her in that appraising manner a man would sometimes use toward a woman when he thought himself unobserved. (Of course, there were some men who did not care whether they were caught openly assessing a lady's attributes or not, but Sir Edmund was definitely not of that number.) However, Cecilia eventually seemed to reach the same conclusion as Sophie about Sir Edmund's lack of interest in her, as any overtures she made in an attempt to capture his attention had all come to nothing. He met these with a polite smile, and more often than not he turned to Sophie and addressed her instead.

Sophie was thankful that Sir Edmund sought her out almost as often as Mr. Maitland did. She found that his presence made Mr. Maitland's attentions less obvious, and Sophie could relax somewhat and not worry that she would suffer the same ignominious fate she had at eighteen should Mr. Maitland fail to commit himself once again. And she was still unsure what answer she would give should he declare himself, so she truly appreciated that because of Sir Edmund's unexpected notice of her she was being granted the freedom to make up her mind at her leisure.

Sophie and the Fosters had been in Bath for nearly a month, and had expanded their acquaintance so much that they were greeted by name nearly everywhere they went. They had formed the habit of going to the Pump Room every morning, and this appeared to be the habit of most of their acquaintance as well. In the evenings there was dancing at the assembly rooms, private dinner parties, or a concert.

It was at the Pump Room one morning that Sophie was introduced to a likely candidate for Sir Edmund's hand.

Miss Emily Woodford was the second-eldest daughter of a gentleman farmer with a large family to settle and so had been sent to live with her grandmother in Bath. She was older than Cecilia but younger than Sophie; Sophie discovered later that she was two-and-twenty. Miss Woodford was not wealthy, and neither was her grandmother; the two women lived very modestly. But Sir Edmund had never mentioned wanting a rich bride, and Sophie did not think, from her and Sir Edmund's earlier conversation, that wealth (or lack thereof) was even a consideration in his choice.

Emily Woodford was not nearly as beautiful as Priscilla Beswick, but she presented a very attractive appearance with her honey-colored hair and dark eyes. And while her clothing was not expensive, it displayed obvious good taste and was well chosen to complement her full figure. Her grandmother, too, seemed a very elegant, pleasant woman, and Sophie felt greatly that these two women possessed far more nobility than Lady Smallpeace or Lady Mary, in spite of the latter pair's rank and titles.

It was Lady Smallpeace who actually introduced Sophie to the Woodfords one morning in the Pump Room. Mrs. and Miss Woodford had nodded at Lady Smallpeace as they walked by but were not stopping to talk until Lady Smallpeace called out to them.

"Wait a moment, Mrs.—" She paused and said in a very audible aside to Lady Mary: "What's her name?" And upon Lady Mary whispering "Woodford," she proceeded to say, just as audibly: "That's it, I remember now. Very rustic," before calling out again: "Mrs. Woodford, Miss Woodford, allow me to introduce you to Miss Lattimore and the Fosters."

Sophie was very surprised by this unexpected bit of condescension on Lady Smallpeace's part, thinking at first it was a kind gesture prompted by a desire to provide Sophie with an amiable acquaintance, but she soon realized it was not meant as a mark of favor but as a way of putting Sophie in her place.

"Miss Lattimore, you will find a lot in common with Miss Woodford. Her father is a country squire, and she, too, is acting as a companion to a female relation," Lady Smallpeace said, introducing the ladies to each other before explaining to the Woodfords that Sophie's aunt Foster "had very generously taken Miss Lattimore into her home." As Lady Mary was once again speaking at the same time as her mother, offering a commentary on how there had been a marked turn in the weather and that morning had been quite unseasonably cool, Lady Smallpeace was almost shouting when she announced that Sophie had been left "with very little income, and had much to be grateful for."

At this point Sophie happened to meet Miss Woodford's eyes, and noticed that she seemed torn between irritation and laughter at Lady Smallpeace and her daughter's antics. There also appeared to be some sympathy in her gaze, as if she understood how it felt always to be labeled "the poor relation." So when Lady Smallpeace just as quickly dismissed the Woodfords after forcing them to stop in the first place, Sophie asked Miss Woodford if she could walk with her.

Miss Woodford's grandmother decided she had walked enough, and a chair was found for her; Miss Woodford offering to bring her a glass of water before heading to the pump with Sophie.

The two young ladies began by exchanging inconsequential but sincere compliments on each other's attire before graduating to a more substantial conversation about Miss Lattimore's impressions of Bath. Mrs. Woodford had been a resident of Bath for many years, so Miss Woodford had frequently come to Bath on visits and was very familiar with the city. She offered to show Miss Lattimore some of her favorite walks, an invitation Sophie readily accepted.

By the end of the morning, a morning spent in traversing the room back and forth in earnest conversation, the two young ladies were quite pleased at having made the acquaintance of someone who seemed destined to become a friend. They even had that most important characteristic of all in common: they counted the same books among their favorites. And when they discovered they were both to attend the Upper Assembly Rooms that evening they promised to look for each other there.

However, a different young lady was the first to find Sophie upon her party's arrival. Priscilla Beswick approached them with quite a few besotted young gentlemen in her wake, whom she graciously introduced to Cecilia before taking Sophie's arm and asking her to walk with her to the tea room.

Sophie, who had hoped to take tea with Miss Woodford, really had no choice in the matter, as Priscilla had turned in that direction before Sophie had even had a chance to respond and was pulling Sophie along with her.

They sat down at a table and Priscilla turned eagerly to Sophie. "Miss Lattimore, have you given any more thought to my situation?"

Sophie *had* thought about it but was sure Priscilla wouldn't be happy with the conclusion she'd reached. "I really feel, Mrs. Beswick, that I should not involve myself in your private affairs any further."

"Call me Priscilla, please. And may I call you Sophia?" Priscilla asked.

"My name is Sophronia." Priscilla wrinkled her perfect little nose in obvious distaste. Sophie sighed. "But call me Sophie, please."

"I knew, after we exchanged confidences the other morning, that we would soon be calling each other by our Christian names!" Priscilla said, a pleased smile on her face. She looked around her, as if to verify there was no one within earshot, before lowering her voice, apparently intent on sharing further secrets. "Sophie, I have thought of something you might do. To help, that is. Since it is your fault I am in this unhappy situation."

Before Sophie could reply she heard her name being called. Looking up, she saw Lady Mary approaching, and

Sophie, for the first time since making Lady Mary's acquaintance, was delighted to see her. She listened happily to her unceasing recital about the temperature of the tea water and felt not the slightest desire to interrupt. "It's tepid, or perhaps you drink it that way, Miss Lattimore," Lady Mary droned on. "Mrs. Beswick, do you prefer a warmer temperature? Or perhaps that would be dangerous. Oh, my, I would hate to think of you scalding yourself. I'm sure that is why the water is not at all hot; it is for our protection. I should not complain if it is not entirely to my taste, because the alternative, well, it does not bear thinking upon, does it, Miss Lattimore?"

Finally, after spending a minute or two blinking in wonder at Lady Mary's avalanche of inanities, Priscilla interrupted her to say, "I beg you to excuse me, but I believe I will return to the assembly rooms. Will you accompany me, Sophie?"

And once again Lady Mary saved Sophie from awkward conversation with Priscilla Beswick by offering to accompany them as well. "For my mother will be looking for me; and really, the tea is not to my taste, though I should not complain."

Priscilla must have realized any opportunity to speak with Sophie had been lost, and she once again cut in on Lady Mary's chatter to say to Sophie, "I will call on you tomorrow morning so we can continue our conversation." She then left Sophie and Lady Mary together and went to find Mr. Andrews, to whom she was promised for the next set.

Sophie was happy to see Miss Woodford as soon as she reentered the assembly rooms. She bid Lady Mary a cordial farewell and left her, having learned over the past few weeks that, as rude and uncomfortable as it might feel, one had to walk away from her while she was still speaking, because she never stopped.

Sophie had just exchanged greetings with Miss and Mrs. Woodford when Sir Edmund suddenly approached to request a dance. Sophie accepted, but first asked to be allowed to present the Woodford ladies to him. She watched Sir Edmund and Miss Woodford carefully as she performed the introduction, but there was no obvious indication from either of them that an event of any significance had occurred. Sophie was not sure if she was relieved or disappointed, but eventually decided that a mere introduction would not fulfill her duty toward Sir Edmund; she had to put forth more effort at matchmaking than that.

So after the dance began and the steps brought Sir Edmund near her, she asked: "What do you think of my friend Miss Woodford? She is very handsome, is she not?"

They were parted before he could reply, but she saw Sir Edmund glance back over at Miss Woodford, as if he had not previously considered the question. When the steps brought them together again he said: "Very handsome. Though in my opinion there is a lovelier lady present."

Sophie did not rate her own attractions very high and would never have presumed that he was speaking of her, and as Mrs. Beswick had joined their set with Mr. Andrews she immediately assumed it was her to whom Sir Edmund referred. "It's true that Mrs. Beswick is without peer, but she is already married," she said, determined to make him aware of Miss Woodford as a potential match.

"The lady I refer to is unmarried." Since this time he accompanied his words with a significant look into Sophie's eyes, she could not fail to grasp his meaning. Before she could respond, however, she was swung onto another dancer's arm, which gave her a few moments to compose herself. And when she returned to Sir Edmund's side, it was almost as if he'd never given her a compliment at all, so quiet and uncomfortable did he seem. Sophie was totally confused. But she was feeling shy as well, so ventured no further conversation. The rest of the dance was performed in silence, though Sophie wondered if there were still messages being conveyed. Did Sir Edmund's hand linger a little longer than was strictly necessary when clasping her own, or was that her imagination? And why did she still feel such a strong attraction to Sir Edmund when she was contemplating accepting Mr. Maitland's suit? It was extremely disconcerting, and she once again thought how funny it was that she had a reputation for her skill at the game of courtship when she was so hopeless at playing it herself.

Though, of course, it wasn't funny at all.

Cecilia was likewise ruminating on the depressing business of making a match. Lord Courtney had become very obvious in his attentions, and they were dancing together at that very moment, but Cecilia knew it was not necessarily in response to her charms but rather because Lady Smallpeace approved of the fact that Cecilia was connected to their family and thus encouraged him in his suit. (Though she wondered that Lady Smallpeace didn't revise her opinion on the importance of sharing a noble bloodline, as Lord Courtney was a rather disappointing specimen and Cecilia sometimes wondered if it was because his parents were *too* closely connected.) Cecilia thought that perhaps Sophie was right in saying that Cecilia did not need to rush into a match with anyone, and such a decision should be based on something other than material or societal prospects. But on the other hand, she had Priscilla Beswick's example before her. Priscilla, who could have married a lord but followed her heart and married a mister instead, had been relegated to country society, like a beautiful flower blooming unseen and unappreciated behind the hedgerows.

Cecilia was proud of herself for this very profound and poetic simile and wondered if she should commit it to paper, but then Lord Courtney accidentally kicked her—just a small kick, nothing serious—and she had to reassure him that he had not hurt her before she could resume her mental meanderings.

Another thing that contradicted Sophie's advice to her, Cecilia thought, was Sophie's own example. If she hadn't caught the fancy of London society with her letter (which could just as easily have earned her their condemnation) and if not for the unfortunate demise of the first Mrs. Maitland, Sophie would have been destined to remain a spinster for the rest of her life. And why? Because she'd failed to make a match during that narrow window of opportunity that had opened in her eighteenth year. Not that it was her fault, of course; Cecilia had nothing but the most sympathetic of feelings toward her cousin and still had difficulty speaking cordially with Mr. Maitland; but it just went to prove that there was a time limit for a young lady in society, and that it behooved Cecilia to make the most of her prospects before that time expired.

The set concluded and Lord Courtney returned Cecilia to her mother's side, where Mr. Hartwell was waiting to dance with her. Cecilia was relieved that she could stop fretting about the future and enjoy her dance with him without having to feel any pressure to reach a decision that she did not want to make. She so appreciated Mr. Hartwell's undemanding company.

Sophie was promised to Mr. Maitland after her dance with Sir Edmund, and if she was forced to compare the two dances she'd have to admit the latter was more enjoyable, as Mr. Maitland smiled at her a great deal more than Sir Edmund had. But then, Mr. Maitland always appeared to be in good spirits. Sophie supposed that was a point in his favor, though sometimes she wondered if a widower and father of two children shouldn't be a *little* more serious.

She'd just had that thought when he became extremely serious indeed. Toward the end of their dance together his smile faded and he asked abruptly, "What is Sir Edmund to you? Is he a suitor?"

And Sophie, annoyed that he felt he had the right to ask her such a question, replied, "I do not know. You would have to ask him. I've made it a point not to assume *anything* where a gentleman is concerned."

She was pleased to see that he appeared to understand her; he looked self-conscious for a moment, but then quickly recovered his usual urbane demeanor. "You are very modest, Sophie. It is obvious the gentleman is smitten with you. How could he not be? You're absolutely adorable."

And she reacted to his admiring gaze and the compliment he'd delivered in a low, seductive tone exactly as he'd probably intended her to: blushing and dropping the subject and not demanding an explanation for his own behavior. She was disconcerted, too, to feel that treacherous ache in her stomach, the physical manifestation of that absurd longing she still had for him.

When they returned to Mrs. Foster they found her in conversation (if it could be called that) with Lady Mary and Lady Smallpeace. Sophie wished she'd noticed them earlier so that she could have avoided them, but since she hadn't she was forced to introduce Mr. Maitland.

He made a very attractive picture as he smiled at the two ladies, and Sophie thought that even Lady Smallpeace could not withstand his charm. And indeed, she had just made that crooked grimace of hers that denoted pleasure when Mr. Maitland made a critical error.

Turning to a strangely silent Lady Mary, he asked if he could have the pleasure of the next dance.

Lady Mary flushed red and her mouth dropped open in surprise, but before she could say aye or nay, Lady Smallpeace had an even more violent reaction. "How impudent! What gall! My daughter, sir, does not dance the *waltz*!" It was obvious that Lady Smallpeace was of that faction of society who considered the waltz a debased and immoral dance.

"I beg your pardon," Mr. Maitland said, still smiling broadly. "I should have realized she did not, or she would have already been on the floor."

Neither Lady Smallpeace nor Lady Mary knew how to reply to this, and both stared at Mr. Maitland as if he were some strange species they had never encountered before. Mr. Maitland merely bowed his goodbyes to the ladies, with a special smile at Sophie, and left them. Sophie then saw him taking the floor with Priscilla Beswick, who looked delighted with her partner, as well she should, for he was undeniably the handsomest and most charming man in the room.

8

*P*riscilla Beswick called on Sophie the next morning, as she'd promised, and Sophie could only regret she had not made a more definite appointment with Miss Woodford. Still, she realized she could not avoid Priscilla indefinitely, and agreed to walk with her to a nearby milliner's shop. So distracted was Priscilla with all of the wares on display that she almost forgot her objective in calling on Sophie, and Sophie had to remind her. On their way back from the shop they passed some gardens, and Sophie suggested to Priscilla that they walk there.

"I am quite tired of walking, Sophie, but if you do wish to walk more, there's a linen draper I wouldn't mind visiting—" Priscilla started to turn back in that direction when Sophie stopped her.

"I just felt we'd have more privacy in the gardens. For our discussion."

"Oh! Oh, of course! Yes! Our *discussion*. I am so glad you reminded me of it. Let us walk in the gardens." Priscilla turned first to her maid, however, asking her to proceed to Miss Lattimore's lodgings on Rivers Street and await her there. Sophie added that she should tell Jonas that Miss Lattimore said to take her to the kitchen and give her whatever she would like.

The maid left and Priscilla went through the gate into the gardens, full of energy now that she'd been reminded of her purpose, and Sophie had to hasten to catch up with her. Priscilla spotted a bench shortly after walking through the gate, and Sophie followed her in that direction.

"Do you think it too dirty to sit?" she asked Sophie, looking suspiciously between her pristine skirts and the bench. Sophie promptly removed a handkerchief from her reticule and dusted off the seat. But when Priscilla still looked at it with a furrowed brow and did not sit, Sophie carefully placed the handkerchief itself on the bench before motioning Priscilla to sit upon it.

"You are so smart, Sophie! You think of everything! Indeed, that is why I thought you were the very one to help me."

Sophie thought it was because she had "ruined" Priscilla's life that she'd been deputized into this unwanted assignment, but she did not intend to remind Priscilla of that. So she merely asked what help Pricilla wanted from her.

"Since you are so good at writing letters, I thought you could write one to Charles." She must have sensed Sophie's immediate negative reaction, because she hurried to add: "Oh, don't worry, he would never have to know it came from you. It would be an anonymous letter, like you're so very fond of writing."

"But why do you not just write Mr. Beswick yourself if you have a message for him?" Sophie asked.

"*I* could not write to Charles. We are not exactly on speaking terms. In our last conversation he told me not to come to Bath."

"And you came anyway?"

"How could I not after he expressly forbade me to do so? I could not let him think he could order me around." At Sophie's expression of disbelief, Priscilla began to look at her a little skeptically. "I must say, Sophie, I'm beginning to doubt you know as much about dealing with gentlemen as you've been rumored to."

"You're absolutely right. My expertise has been highly exaggerated," Sophie assured her.

Priscilla was stymied, but just for a moment. "Oh, well, between the two of us we can manage it, I'm sure. I can give you the general idea to convey, and then you can write it up in your elegant manner. Of that I have no doubt you're capable, as I've seen an example of your work," Priscilla said a little grimly, and Sophie realized this would be a bone of contention between them for some time yet.

"What is the 'general idea' you want to convey?" Sophie asked, deciding to avoid the bigger question for the moment of whether or not she would be participating.

"Well, I thought if you explained to him how popular I

was here, that all of the gentlemen were lining up to dance with me . . . You know," Priscilla said, "paint a picture of why he should come to Bath as soon as possible."

"Make him jealous, in other words," Sophie suggested.

"Exactly!" Priscilla said, pleased. "Perhaps you are not as ignorant as I thought." She said this as if she were conveying a great compliment, and Sophie supposed a woman who thought being compared to a cow was romantic probably considered telling someone they were not completely ignorant was high praise indeed. "So you will write the letter?" Priscilla asked.

"I think we should reconsider your strategy," Sophie said, then continued before Priscilla could voice a protest. "If Charles has half a brain he already knows all that you intend me to say. I do not think receiving an anonymous letter telling him his wife is popular with other gentlemen will motivate him to race to your side. Either he'll be angry that you continue to defy him or he'll suspect *you* of being the anonymous letter-writer. Whichever he believes, it will make him even more determined to stay away."

Priscilla's disappointed expression changed to one of awed respect. "I believe the rumors are correct after all. You *do* understand gentlemen."

Sophie thought a more ironic statement had never been made, yet she wasn't about to contradict Priscilla and have her doubting her again. "I am older than you and have spent much of that time in observation. I know more than a little about human behavior. This is what you should do . . ."

They returned to the house on Rivers Street and, finding that the Foster ladies had left for the Pump Room, decided to write the letter there. By this time Sophie had convinced Priscilla that there was no point in Sophie writing the letter; it had to come from Priscilla herself. Although Priscilla ostensibly agreed to this, after she'd ruined two sheets of paper and complained loudly and at length of the possibility of staining her clothes or hands with ink, Sophie ended up writing the letter for her. However, once Sophie announced she was finished, Priscilla willingly put down the copy of *The Lady's Magazine* she had been perusing while Sophie labored over the letter and signed her name to it with a flourish.

Priscilla looked at it with satisfaction. "I think we have done quite a good job of this, Sophie," she said, though she'd actually contributed very little, if anything at all. "Charles cannot fail to come now."

"And I expressed your feelings correctly? You do miss him and long for his company, and regret that you parted in anger?"

"Oh, of course. Everything you said sounded marvelous. Though I do wonder—"

Sophie leaned forward and took the letter from Priscilla, hoping it wasn't going to be too difficult to edit. "Yes?" she prompted.

"Do you think Charles would have preferred the bonnet with the embroidered net? Perhaps I should have purchased it instead of the Cambridge hat with ostrich feathers."

And that's when Sophie began to realize this letter was going to cause her just as many problems as the original.

Though Priscilla might annoy her at times, Sophie was developing a fondness for her. She thought Priscilla was rather like a mischievous kitten: you never knew if it was more likely to hiss or purr at you if you reached out to pet it, but it was adorable in either attitude. However, the next morning Sophie had an outing with Miss Woodford and had to admit to herself that she enjoyed it far more. They, too, went for a walk, but to the circulating library rather than the milliner, and instead of an unhappy marriage, they discussed books and plays and music. Sophie learned a lot about Miss Woodford's brothers and sisters and envied her greatly, as it sounded as if life in a country house with four siblings had much to recommend it, even if it did mean there was less money to go around.

So caught up did they become in each other's conversation that they were taken completely by surprise when it began to rain as they were walking up and down Milsom Street, peering unseeingly into the shop windows. Neither had brought an umbrella and the rain had grown quite heavy, so by unspoken consent they rushed in through the nearest shop door, taking no notice of what it might be. They were surprised to find themselves inside a bootmaker's, and one that served a primarily masculine clientele, or at least was doing so at the moment that they ran in breathless and damp, to the delight of the gentlemen shopping there.

Sophie and Emily (as they had begun calling each other) stood for a moment as if paralyzed, while one of the bolder men made a jest that it was raining lovely young ladies. The two women turned to leave but were dismayed when they looked out at the sheets of rain that now appeared to be falling at an intensity that made any thought of venturing out almost impossible.

Then Sophie heard a familiar voice. "Miss Lattimore, may I be of assistance?"

She turned to find Mr. Hartwell there, looking more angelic than ever in the dark and humid shop, an expression of concern on his face.

"Oh, Mr. Hartwell! How very good to see you," Sophie said enthusiastically, and Mr. Hartwell blushed a little, something he was prone to do since his coloring was so fair. "Are you acquainted with Miss Woodford?"

And Sophie was once again brought to a realization of her complete and total ignorance of that strange alchemy that was physical attraction. For while Emily had met Sir Edmund two evenings before with no change of manner at all, an introduction to the less dashing Mr. Hartwell appeared to discompose her greatly.

Emily started to give him her hand, then withdrew it before he could take it, curtsying instead and nearly losing her balance, so that Sophie reached out a hand to steady her. But Mr. Hartwell was faster, taking Emily's arm and saying, "Careful, Miss Woodford. The floor is slippery from the rain."

An expression of adoration suffused Emily's face and she said, "Thank you, Mr. Hartwell. It is *such* a pleasure to meet you."

Sophie, who had just been speaking with her for hours, was quite alarmed to hear this response uttered in a soft, gushing tone she'd never once heard during any of their prior conversations. Mr. Hartwell turned even redder and cleared his throat. He carefully removed his hand from Emily's arm and took a few steps back before turning to address Sophie. "Perhaps if I found you ladies a chair?" he suggested.

"Oh, could you?" Sophie asked. "But I'd hate for you to have to go out in this—" She finished the sentence with a gesture toward the window.

"I think my hat can withstand the elements far more easily than yours," Mr. Hartwell said with a grin. And indeed, Sophie had just that moment blown at a bedraggled piece of lace that had fallen from her bonnet into her face. "You ladies wait here." He then looked around at the gentlemen who were watching the scene with great interest. "No one will bother you," he said in a menacing tone, and the men immediately shifted their gazes away from the ladies and tried to appear busy.

"Should you not wait a moment or two, until the rain lets up a trifle?" Emily asked Mr. Hartwell.

But in the few minutes they had been talking the rain had lessened, at least enough so that it no longer resembled a deluge of biblical proportions. "Thank you for your concern, Miss Woodford. I believe that it *has* improved somewhat," Mr. Hartwell said, smiling at her. Miss Emily Woodford was quite tall, and Mr. Hartwell was only an inch or two taller, so Sophie wondered if that was why Emily seemed able to stare so intently into his eyes. Sophie was actually growing more than a little uncomfortable, but it might have been the heated and crowded interior of the shop that made her so, and not the warmth emanating from her friend.

Sophie could not tell if Mr. Hartwell was experiencing a reciprocal attraction; he was acting in the same gentlemanly and courteous manner he always did. Sophie also knew him to be genuinely enamored of Cecilia and did not think he was the type to lightly transfer his affections to another lady. In fact, she felt she should warn Emily before her attraction grew into something more or she embarrassed herself by displaying too obvious a partiality in public. So when Mr. Hartwell finally left and Emily turned to her and said, "What a kind gentleman!" Sophie agreed, telling her, "Yes, he is always extremely accommodating. He is one of my cousin Cecilia's suitors."

But Emily appeared more confused than disappointed. "I don't understand," she said. "I thought your cousin was entertaining Lord Courtney's suit."

"Yes, well, my cousin is still quite young," Sophie began, before realizing there was really no explanation she could offer for Cecilia's behavior, and that all of the gentlemen appeared to have stopped what they were doing to eavesdrop on her conversation with Emily. Sophie decided a change of subject was in order and began a discussion about needlework, which was sure to be of little interest to the men who surrounded them, and was of hardly any interest to her or Emily, either, but served to pass the time until the chairs arrived.

The next evening Sophie's aunt and cousin had plans to attend a concert in the company of Lady Smallpeace and her family. Since Mrs. Foster was going, Sophie was not needed in the role of chaperone, but as a single relation her choice was either to accompany her relatives or stay at home, and so she chose to attend the event in the hope of finding more congenial company there.

She purposely hung back as seats were found for the members of their party. Cecilia was flanked by Lord Courtney and her mother, who sat next to Lady Smallpeace. Lady Mary was next to Lord Courtney, so Sophie chose the seat on the side of Lady Mary, which did not have the best view of the musicians, but was on the end of a bench so made for an easy escape, if necessary. There was also enough room there for someone to sit next to her; if someone desired to, that is. Sophie was not sure who it was *she* desired to sit there until, while looking up from the printed program, she spotted Sir Edmund strolling into the room.

She could not prevent the sudden look of delight that crossed her face and hoped that she could compose herself before he saw it, but as if drawn by her gaze he immedi-

ately looked in her direction. He smiled and started walking toward her, then hesitated and looked to see with
whom she was seated. She decided some encouragement
would not be amiss, as at that moment she made the firm
decision that there was no one she desired to take the place
next to her more than Sir Edmund. So she nodded eagerly
at him, in a gesture she hoped would make it obvious she
was inviting him to come speak to her.

He started forward again and bowed as he reached her,
saying, "Good evening. Is this seat available?"

"Indeed it is. You are welcome to take it," Sophie replied, and Sir Edmund sat down. Lady Mary noticed his
presence and he nodded to her, but Sophie was relieved
when she turned back to her conversation with Lord
Courtney after merely returning Sir Edmund's nod.

"You do not think there will be . . . talk, if I sit here
with you?" Sir Edmund asked, in such a low tone that Sophie was forced to incline her head toward him a little in
order to hear him. When she realized what he'd said and
how close she was to him, she hastily moved back, accidentally jostling Lady Mary and having to beg her pardon.

She turned again to Sir Edmund, but some of her pleasure in his company had been diminished by his words.
She felt both her "suitors" (if that's what either of them
were) had much to learn about courting a woman. Mr.
Maitland paid too *little* heed to society's opinion and Sir Edmund too much. "'Talk,' Sir Edmund?" she asked. "When
we are merely sitting next to each other on a bench at a
public concert?"

"Have I offended you? I beg your pardon. This is why I sought your advice to begin with, if you recall," Sir Edmund said. "I am hopeless in my interactions with ladies."

Sophie wondered if she'd been too guarded thus far as well. She was still uncertain if he desired anything more from her than friendship, but how was he to know she would welcome a warmer relationship if she did not convey that to him? He was the only man, other than Frederick Maitland, for whom she'd ever felt such a strong attraction, but in contrast to Mr. Maitland, she also *liked* him so very much. She decided to throw caution to the winds. "Are you saying, Sir Edmund, that you wish to learn to *flirt*?"

Sir Edmund looked surprised for a moment, but then a definite gleam of interest lit his eyes. "Are you offering to teach me?" he asked, lowering his voice even further so as not to be heard by Lady Mary. Sophie's stomach began to flutter in reaction to that husky tone, and the thought occurred to her that she was playing with fire. She suddenly felt very alone with him in their corner of the darkened hall, the flickering candlelight gently highlighting the planes of his face and glinting in his eyes. She always found him attractive, as she'd just acknowledged to herself, but tonight in his evening clothes, speaking throatily and intimately in a low voice, Sophie felt a little like a fragile moth fluttering around a flame, about to have its wings singed. But she was finished being too cautious, she reminded herself.

"I think you are more skilled than you pretend, Sir Edmund," she finally replied, after the silence between them had grown unbearably loud in Sophie's ears, filled as it was with the thumping of her heart.

"But I am a novice at the art, Miss Lattimore. I place myself entirely in your hands," he said, his expression displaying awareness of his double entendre and contradicting his assertion of being an innocent at this game.

"You are a fast learner," Sophie praised him. "Still, your inexperience betrays you. A true proficient would have asked to share the lady's concert bill."

They both looked down at the paper in her lap. "What if I had one of my own?" he asked, a note of humor reverberating in his soft voice.

"Do you?" Sophie asked.

There was a rustling sound, as Sir Edmund deliberately folded his program and put it in his waistcoat pocket. "I seem to have misplaced my program, Miss Lattimore. Might I share yours?"

Sophie was a trifle alarmed by her own audacity thus far but was not about to draw back now. She shifted closer to Sir Edmund on the bench, holding the program between them, and he bent his head nearer her own. She could feel gentle puffs of his breath teasing the curls on her cheek and neck, and his leg was brushing hers. She completely forgot that *she* was supposed to be tutoring *him*.

"And what do I do next, Fair Instructress?" he whispered into her ear.

Sophie could not think of a single thing, or at least she could think of nothing that she wanted him to do that was appropriate between an unbetrothed couple in a public setting. She was not even sure if she *could* speak, so overcome was she by his nearness. Finally she managed to whisper, "Perhaps you could comment on the delights the evening has in store."

"You mean those listed on the concert bill, or as embodied in the charms of my companion?" he asked. And though his voice faltered a little, as if he, too, was finding it difficult to converse in a natural manner, Sophie felt it unfair that he was able to respond more quickly than she was.

She could not have said whether the program was even written in English, the words appeared such a jumbled mishmash before her eyes. But apparently Sir Edmund could read it and endeavored to see it even more clearly, because he reached out to take a corner of it, his hand touching hers as he did so.

Sophie was so agitated and excited that when the music began at just that moment she jumped in surprise, startling Lady Mary.

"Oh, Sir Edmund," Lady Mary said, noticing the two of them sharing the slip of paper. "You do not have a program. Take mine, please, I can share with my cousin." And she shoved the unwanted program into his hand, chattering all the while, until someone behind them cleared his throat.

Sir Edmund waited a moment after Lady Mary had turned away, then whispered to Sophie: "It is your turn to misplace yours." Sophie, her senses overstimulated by the music and his nearness, did not respond in words, but leaned back until she could rest her shoulder against his. It almost felt as if he were embracing her, as he had shifted in his seat so that his arm was behind her back, and they sat that way, Sophie feeling more cherished than she had in years, for most of the evening. Occasionally his hand or foot would brush hers, and she would feel a delightful tingle in response. She was far more conscious of him than of the music, and on the carriage ride home with her aunt and cousin she could not bring herself to offer one intelligent opinion about the concert, though she'd never enjoyed one more.

9

*S*ophie had been surprised that Mr. Maitland was not at the concert or, indeed, anywhere to be found in recent days. She did not think she could have flirted with Sir Edmund so brazenly under Mr. Maitland's knowing gaze, and so did not know if she regretted his absence or was grateful for it. She sometimes felt as fickle as Cecilia, keeping two men dangling at the same time, but the difference was that she was genuinely drawn to both Mr. Maitland and Sir Edmund, while Cecilia could barely tolerate Lord Courtney. Another difference was that Cecilia was sure of Mr. Hartwell's intentions, while Sophie was sure of nothing at all. Sophie was worried that if she did make an effort to attach Sir Edmund, she might lose Mr. Maitland and wind up with no one, as it was possible Sir Edmund had no romantic intentions toward her. The one thing Sophie *was* sure of was that she was done living as a poor relation and lonely spinster. She was determined to end her stay in Bath with an engagement. She was just not sure to which gentleman.

While she had greatly enjoyed herself at the pump concert the other evening, she now worried it had been a terrible mistake to offer to tutor Sir Edmund in dalliance. For if he continued to flirt with her, how was she to know if it was all an act or if he genuinely cared? She felt ridiculous, too, offering *him* instruction in romance, as if she believed herself to be a modern-day Circe. There was nothing more pathetic than an aging spinster putting on airs, particularly when Sir Edmund was so very good-looking and obviously needed no guidance from *her* on how to make himself appealing to women. So when she thought back on that evening, as she frequently did, she was torn between feelings of humiliation and exhilaration.

It did not help matters that during their one meeting since the concert she and Sir Edmund had each been shy of the other. It was true, however, that the circumstances of the two encounters were vastly different, as the second was not in a darkened concert hall but in the Pump Room during the brightest part of the day, where they were surrounded by takers of water and tellers of gossip.

Sophie was walking with Emily Woodford when she spotted Sir Edmund. Sophie was becoming quite fond of Emily, particularly since Sophie had done her duty by introducing her to Sir Edmund and Emily had been so good as to *not* fall in love with him. But Sophie would have thought even more highly of her if, when Sir Edmund joined them, Emily had recalled an urgent appointment and left Sophie and Sir Edmund to walk alone together. Because Sophie was convinced that much of Sir Edmund's restraint that morning was caused by Emily's presence.

Since Emily didn't suddenly acquire miraculous mind-reading powers and leave, Sophie determined that she would try to make her and Sir Edmund more comfortable with each other. And she was succeeding in drawing them both out when Emily happened upon the very subject that caused *Sophie* to feel least comfortable of all.

They were discussing local entertainments and Emily asked Sir Edmund if he had attended the concert at the Upper Assembly Rooms the previous evening. "I know you were there, Sophie, though I did not see you again after you left the Octagon Room. Were you able to attend, Sir Edmund?"

"I was," he said, with a sideways glance at Sophie. "I enjoyed it very much."

Sophie felt herself blushing but met Sir Edmund's gaze for a moment, and they shared a secret smile.

"Which did you enjoy more, the Italian or the German composers?" Emily asked, to Sophie's consternation. She had not thought she would be quizzed on the content of the concert to which she'd paid absolutely no attention.

Sir Edmund rescued her by saying he was partial to Pleyel and asked Emily her favorite. Thankfully Emily could talk at length about music, and Sir Edmund and Sophie allowed her to chatter away on the subject while peeking at each other from time to time to see if the other was looking before glancing away in embarrassment at being caught doing so.

The secret of Mr. Maitland's absence was revealed the next day when he called upon the ladies at their lodgings. He was not their only caller; the drawing room was full at the time, and after paying his respects to Mrs. Foster he greeted Lady Smallpeace and Lady Mary, who responded as dissimilarly as they always did, Lady Smallpeace appearing affronted and offering terse proclamations, and Lady Mary reacting with blushing confusion and meandering sentences.

Mr. Hartwell and Lord Courtney were also present, as was Mrs. Beswick, and Mr. Maitland seemed at first to have called on purpose to see Priscilla, as he gave her his attention next and seemed completely delighted with her company. Sophie, who was attempting to draw Lord Courtney's attention away from Cecilia so that Mr. Hartwell might converse with her, was finding it such a difficult task that she did not think to feel offended by Mr. Maitland's neglect. When he eventually made his way to her side, her primary emotion was surprise, so distracted was she by Cecilia's stupidity in entertaining Lord Courtney's suit and thereby alienating Mr. Hartwell's affections.

Still, she did wonder where Mr. Maitland had gone and was happy to have him assuage her curiosity, though she felt he could have done so in a less provoking manner.

"Did you miss me?" he asked, looking meltingly into her eyes.

"I cried for days," she replied drily, and he laughed, as she meant him to, but there was an underlying awkwardness between them, as they both couldn't help being reminded of the last time he'd left without a word, and how she really *had* cried for days, if not months.

"I went to Wiltshire. I have a tidy little farm there. Bought it after my marriage," he said, before continuing quickly, as if he realized the best way to woo her was not with reminders of his past betrayal. "The children usually stay there with their nurse, but I brought them back with me to Bath."

Sophie just blinked, not sure what this was meant to portend. "Did you?" she finally asked, as she felt it a nice, neutral response.

"I did. To meet you," he added softly, after a quick look around to ensure no one else was listening.

"I am sure that I will be delighted to meet them. We all will," she said, trying to make the gesture less pointed in its significance.

Mr. Maitland looked at her without speaking for a moment. "You are not going to make this easy for me, are you, Sophie?" he finally asked, before giving her a slight, self-assured smile. It was dangerous, that smile, as was the light in his eyes. "I do not mind, though. I relish the thought of winning you. My treasure," he said tenderly, and now Sophie was the one to look around them in fear of observers. Because this seemed far more serious than flirtation, and she was suddenly panic-stricken that if Mr. Maitland continued behaving toward her this way in public, she would no longer have the luxury of choosing her fate. Her fate would be sealed.

Someone had observed them, she discovered later, when all the guests had left and her aunt had gone to her room and only Sophie and her cousin were left in the drawing room together.

"I beg your pardon, Sophie, if you think it impertinent of me to ask, but are things settled between you and Mr. Maitland?" Cecilia said.

Sophie, looking over at Cecilia, noticed she appeared pale and wan. Sophie did not think she was enjoying Bath very much these days. Sophie wasn't surprised, as Cecilia spent much of her time with Lady Smallpeace and Lord Courtney, who were not the most congenial of companions.

"Settled? Do you mean are we betrothed?" Sophie asked, and Cecilia nodded. "No, of course not. Surely you do not think I would enter into a secret engagement? If I become engaged, I will be sure to announce it in the papers, you can have no doubt." Sophie said this last jokingly, though she was making a pretense of lightheartedness, as her heart had sunk at Cecilia's question.

"His attentions seem . . . so very pointed. Surely you still do not doubt that he will offer for you?" Cecilia asked.

"I will have some doubt until he actually does, I suppose, but you are right that he appears to be serious this time."

"And have you decided what your answer will be?"

Sophie sighed. "I have decided . . . that I am completely undecided," she said, smiling ruefully. "If he offers for me and he hasn't already provided an explanation of his past behavior, I will demand one before I give my answer. But for some reason the thought of committing myself fills me with panic—even though I'd once thought I could be offered no greater joy than to become his wife."

"I understand completely," Cecilia said. "I am also panic-stricken at the thought of committing myself to an engagement."

They were silent for a moment. Sophie studied Cecilia as she stared unseeingly at a portrait of an unknown lady in a ruff that had come with the house, and thought again that she'd never seen her usually happy-go-lucky cousin so dejected. She longed to talk to Cecilia but was worried that if she did not choose her words carefully, they could spur Cecilia on to the wrong course of action. And Sophie was conscious, too, that she was not setting the best example for her younger cousin while her own romantic affairs were so tangled. Still, she had to try.

"I have no wish to pry, either, but is it an engagement to Lord Courtney that causes you to feel panic-stricken?" Sophie asked.

Cecilia nodded.

"Cecilia, if you are so unhappy at even the prospect of marriage to him, why do you continue to encourage his suit?"

Apparently these were not the correct words, as Cecilia's

spine straightened and she frowned at Sophie. "You must be aware, Cousin, that he is the catch of my generation."

"I am aware of it, and it is complete and utter nonsense. Why? Because he is rich? Because three hundred years ago some pox-ridden king was bribed into giving his ancestor a title? You will be living with a *man*, Cecilia. Not his money or title."

"You're one to give *me* advice. Do you think I've not seen how you are encouraging Sir Edmund's suit at the same time you dangle Mr. Maitland on a string? You're playing a dangerous game, Sophie, so I would warn you to look to your own affairs before you criticize mine!"

Cecilia stormed out of the drawing room, and Sophie was left with the lady in the ruff. She turned to the portrait. "I hope I didn't insult one of your relatives just now. And perhaps I underestimated how many years ago the pox-ridden king gave Lord Courtney's ancestor his title. Lady Smallpeace could enlighten me, I'm sure."

Then, realizing it wasn't quite the thing to be conversing with an inanimate object, Sophie also left the drawing room.

Before Sophie could meet Mr. Maitland's children, she was honored by a different introduction. Mr. Beswick had arrived in Bath, and Priscilla brought him around to Rivers Street the next day. She first sent a note to Sophie asking permission to call, and as Cecilia and Mrs. Foster had their usual appointment with their friends in the Pump

Room, Sophie told them to go without her and that she would stay behind to receive the Beswicks.

She was a trifle worried that Mr. Beswick would be angry with her for her interference in his affairs, as she did not know if he counted it a blessing or a curse that he had won Priscilla's hand in marriage, particularly considering Priscilla's behavior since. But when he and Priscilla were ushered into the drawing room, his mood, though not exactly pleasant, did not appear to be caused by resentment of Sophie, but rather by the necessity for him to travel to Bath.

Sophie had only seen Charles Beswick once before, in a poorly lit ballroom for no more than a few minutes, and would probably not have recognized him had she passed him on the street. Now that she had the time to study his appearance, she found that he had the look of a gentleman farmer, or at least of someone who spent much of his time out-of-doors. His complexion was tanned, and he wore his shirt and jacket collars lower than any other gentleman of Sophie's acquaintance. Still, he was not *un*fashionable. His informal, nonchalant air made him appear as if he cared nothing for the opinion of others, thereby setting his own fashion.

But he certainly did not seem as if he belonged at Priscilla's side, as she always looked as if she'd stepped out of an illustration from the pages of *La Belle Assemblée*. Today she was even more glamorous than usual, but her efforts seemed to be lost on Mr. Beswick, who did not seem to recognize or care that Priscilla was wearing the latest in *à la modality*.

They also did not appear to have resolved their differences. After Priscilla had presented Sophie to Mr. Beswick and Sophie had encouraged her guests to sit, an awkward, tense silence pervaded the room. The situation was not improved when Sophie asked Mr. Beswick how long they were to have the pleasure of his company in Bath.

"Pleasure! Ha!" Mr. Beswick pronounced, to Sophie's surprise and dismay. Priscilla rushed in to try to smooth things over.

"Charles has an unreasonable prejudice against Bath, though he's never even stayed here for more than two days."

"It's overcrowded and very inconvenient for keeping a carriage."

"There are some fine walks, I believe," Sophie offered.

"I much prefer to ride," said Charles.

"I told Charles that once he has been to an entertainment at the Upper Assembly Rooms or taken the waters in the Pump Room, he will grow to love it here as much as the rest of us do," Priscilla said.

Sophie did not think that either of those two excursions would succeed in changing Mr. Beswick's negative opinion of Bath. But just as Sophie was sure she was destined to take him into irrevocable dislike, Mr. Beswick seemed to shake off his bad humor. He smiled affectionately at Priscilla and said, "Ah, Pris, I thought you knew me better than that."

Priscilla blushed at this comment and smiled adoringly back at him, and Sophie entertained the hope that the couple might be closer to a reconciliation than she had assumed.

But then Mr. Beswick continued, "I have no intention of going to either of those places."

Sophie felt that her comparison of Priscilla Beswick to a mischievous kitten had never been more apt, as she wrinkled her lovely little nose and her fingers suddenly curled and took on the appearance of paws. Sophie hurried to intercede, saying: "Mr. Beswick, please do not dismiss the area's attractions so quickly. I presume you are a gentleman who prefers sporting activities. Priscilla has a large circle of friends here in Bath, some whose tastes are similar to yours. I am sure we can arrange for some excursions that you would enjoy."

Charles seemed disposed to accept this olive branch, inclining his head toward Sophie. Priscilla, however, looked disappointed and said: "But . . . I'd much prefer dancing."

Charles' disgruntled expression reappeared at this remark, and Sophie quicky began an innocuous conversation about the weather, feeling a sudden sympathy for Lady Mary as she did so.

Sophie's next introduction, to Mr. Maitland's children, was a much grander and more public affair. Mr. Maitland had arranged for a breakfast at Sydney Gardens, with tea, cold meat, and pastries to be served in a private supper box. Obviously Sophie could not be the only person present outside of Mr. Maitland's family and the children's nurse, nor did she wish to spend the day tête-à-tête with them. So Mr. Maitland had also invited both of the Foster ladies and their noble friends. Lady Smallpeace declined the invitation for herself, as she didn't really feel like showing such condescension to a mere "Mr. Maitland" of nowhere in particular, who could not name any relatives of whom Lady Smallpeace had ever heard. But surprisingly, Lady Mary and Lord Courtney did accept the invitation and were in attendance, as were Priscilla and Charles Beswick. Sophie very astutely guessed that Mr. Maitland had invited Priscilla before learning of her husband's arrival and couldn't withdraw the invitation after discovering she would be bringing him along. Though Sophie now believed Mr. Maitland was truly fond of her and a proposal from him seemed imminent, she also knew he enjoyed the company of ladies far more than that of gentlemen. Particularly ladies who were lovely to look at, like Priscilla was.

And Priscilla had outdone herself. She was always dressed to the nines, of course, but her outfit that day could have been displayed in an art gallery and people would have paid admission to see it. Her dress and matching spencer were a vibrant green, a color which couldn't have been more flattering to her hair and eyes. The spencer was lined with black silk, and above its collar was another collar of stand-up white lace that framed her face. But it was her hat that stole the show, and she had wisely kept the rest of her outfit relatively simple so that the hat could take center stage. It was a black velvet toque with intricate cording also in black, and egret feathers of black and green waved proudly above it. Pinned to one side was a small round white aigrette with a spray of green berries.

Sophie thought it the most beautiful hat she'd ever seen but wondered that Priscilla had chosen to wear it on a trip to the gardens. A bandeau held it to her head, but it had no ribbons, which made Sophie think Priscilla would have to be very careful to hold on to it if there were any gusty winds.

Likewise, Priscilla's slippers, while dainty and a pretty green to match her dress, did not look like the most comfortable choice for walking, and Sophie was glad she'd chosen to wear sturdy half boots and her favorite straw bonnet, even if her outfit did pale in comparison to Priscilla Beswick's.

Mr. Maitland had invited one other single gentleman, Mr. Andrews, so that the ladies would not completely outnumber the men. Of the four gentlemen present, Mr. Beswick was the only one who was not completely outshone by Mr. Maitland in physical attractiveness, and he was married. Though Sophie did not know if Mr. Maitland had arranged matters this way on purpose, she couldn't deny that in contrast with Lord Courtney and Mr. Andrews, Mr. Maitland appeared the pinnacle of masculine perfection, the beau of every woman's dreams.

Sir Edmund had most definitely *not* been invited. Sophie told herself she was very glad Sir Edmund was not present. She needed to forget him entirely and overcome this strange craving she had for his company. It was Mr. Maitland she wanted and had wanted since she was eighteen. Wasn't it? Hadn't she? Good gracious, she still did not know. She hoped that after this day she would finally have the answer.

Sophie tried to calm her nervousness at the thought of meeting Mr. Maitland's children, telling herself that she shouldn't endue the occasion with too much significance or she would not be able to behave naturally. (Already she viewed the excursion as one might a trip to the dentist.) But when she and the Fosters had arrived at the pleasure gardens most of the party was already present, and there was such a bustle of finding seats and greeting one another that Sophie was able to relax a little, grateful that there were so many invited that she could fade into the background.

The children were with their nurse, seemingly indifferent to the presence of the other adults around them. Sophie had already learned from Mr. Maitland that his daughter Jane was six years old and her little brother Frederick, named for his father, was three. Freddie was very like Mr. Maitland, as he was already a handsome child, with his father's sparkling blue eyes and a precocious smile. Sophie was not at all surprised as the day progressed to find him very capable of manipulating the ladies present, including her, into giving him whatever his little heart desired.

His sister was not nearly as handsome or charming. Sophie was no expert on children, but she thought Jane seemed very small and thin for her age, with a pinched and wan face and a pettish disposition. When Sophie had learned of the children from Mr. Maitland she had imagined that when she and Jane met they would be drawn to each other immediately, as she assumed a little girl would especially miss her mother and be happy to have an older female friend. And while it was true that Jane was drawn to an older female, unfortunately that female was not Sophie.

Mr. Maitland had introduced all of them very casually to the children, gesturing to where they sat in the corner with their nurse and announcing to no one in particular, "That scamp over there is Frederick, and the little miss is Jane." People nodded and smiled and Priscilla exclaimed, "What a handsome little boy! He is a miniature version of you, Mr. Maitland. How very quaint!"

Sophie winced at this remark, as she was sure poor Jane had heard it often and must be sensitive to the fact that her brother received all the attention. So she approached the little girl, kneeling down and saying, "It is so nice to meet you, Miss Jane. My, what a pretty reticule that is. May I see it?" Sophie held out her hand, thinking to just take the reticule for a moment and give it back after admiring it briefly, but Jane looked at her like she was the devil incarnate and yelled, "No!" before turning away from Sophie and burying her face in her nurse's skirts.

The nurse immediately chided the little girl, who then began to cry, and Sophie was forced to intervene, saying, "Oh, no, do not scold her, please." She could not recall ever feeling so embarrassed in her life and was not sure how to extricate herself from her predicament.

The situation was somewhat improved by Freddie pointing at her and shouting, "Pretty lady!" (He resembled his father more and more with every passing minute.) Grateful that at least one of the children liked her, Sophie smiled at him and said, "Thank you, kind sir," before standing and moving away from the nursery party. It was obvious the others were embarrassed for her as well, and Cecilia tried to deflect attention away from the incident by commenting on the likelihood of the rain holding off for the remainder of the day, but her efforts were nullified when Lord Courtney said loudly, "The girl probably thought Miss Lattimore meant to steal her purse."

Mr. Maitland seemed totally unaffected by the incident, behaving as if nothing unpleasant had happened and generally acting as if the children were not present. Sophie huddled in her seat, wishing she were anywhere but where she was, and did not contribute anything to the conversation. Her humiliation was complete when Jane, having recovered from her crying fit, ventured over to Lady Mary and handed *her* the reticule, saying, "*You* can hold it." This was pronounced with a triumphant look in Sophie's direction and the first smile Sophie had seen on the child's face.

10

Jane spent the rest of the day at Lady Mary's side, though her nurse did try to remove her, certain that the six-year-old must be annoying the noblewoman. However, Lady Mary assured her she was happy to spend time with Jane, and she did look gratified by the little girl's obvious preference for her company.

After the group had finished their breakfast, Mr. Maitland asked what they would like to do next. "Perhaps a walk through the Labyrinth? Miss Lattimore?"

Sophie looked up to see him holding out his arm to her. She assumed he planned to leave his children in the supper box, and she was pleased at the opportunity to remove herself from the scene of her humiliation. But it felt rather forward to leave the rest of the party and scamper off with Mr. Maitland. "I would be happy to," Sophie said. "Would anyone else care to join us?"

She placed her hand on his arm as the Beswicks began debating whether they wanted to walk. Priscilla at first had no interest in such exertion, claiming it was far too hot, but Charles told her he had no plans to sit and eat Bath buns and drink tea the rest of the afternoon. "And the walk would do you good," he said. "You used to be a prodigious walker and now you barely take ten steps a day."

"But . . . a labyrinth," Priscilla protested, her eyes big. "What if we were to get lost?"

Mr. Maitland triumphantly waved a piece of paper in the air. "I purchased a map at the bar."

"How clever of you!" Priscilla said, clasping her hands in front of her bosom.

"It's a very pleasant walk, and there's a swing in the center," Sophie told her.

"Merlin's swing, to be precise," Mr. Maitland said. "I intended to ride it with Miss Lattimore, but four can fit comfortably."

"Merlin," Beswick said, his bored expression changing to one of excitement. "I've seen some of his other mechanical contrivances. And he designed this swing, you say? I'd be very interested in seeing it."

Mr. Beswick had never appeared to greater advantage than he did now, with a look of good-natured eagerness and intelligence on his face, and Sophie could understand why Priscilla had fallen in love with him when she saw him like this. She only hoped Priscilla was looking at her husband as admiringly as she had Mr. Maitland.

Mr. Maitland turned to the other guests to make some

suggestions for their enjoyment before the foursome set off on their walk. And for the first time, Sophie began to take some enjoyment in the day and her surroundings.

She really did love Sydney Gardens, though she'd only managed to visit a few times since she'd arrived in Bath, as Aunt Foster preferred the Pump Room. And she had yet to attend one of their gala nights, where apparently there were fireworks and other spectacular entertainments. While exploring the gardens with her cousin, Sophie had seen a pavilion that could have come from ancient Greece, an iron bridge in the Chinese style that spanned the canal, and even a sham castle complete with a moat. Sophie and Cecilia had also ventured into the Labyrinth, although they had not tried the swing. There was a fee for both, and even though it was only a few shillings, Sophie hadn't felt she'd had the time for it on her previous visit.

And walking through the Labyrinth with a handsome male suitor was infinitely more exciting than traversing it with her cousin. She was almost sorry she had invited the Beswicks to accompany them.

Mr. Maitland, though, seemed undaunted by their company. Priscilla Beswick, however much of a walker she'd been in the past, did not seem very adept at the art now, and Mr. Maitland easily put some distance between them and the Beswicks, enough that he could speak in a low voice to Sophie without fear of being overheard.

"So what do you think of my children? Jane bears an unfortunate resemblance to her mother, poor girl, but Freddie's a taking little thing, wouldn't you agree?"

Sophie was not sure exactly how to respond to this, as it seemed to be an implied insult of both his dead wife and his daughter. And her heart sank at the necessity of stating outright how unpopular she was with the little girl. "Freddie *is* an extremely handsome child, but you must have noticed that Jane took me in dislike," she said.

Mr. Maitland dismissed this with a wave of his hand and a short laugh. "I told you she takes after her mother, didn't I? She dislikes all attractive females. I think she's worried about me taking a new wife. She'll come around in time."

"She seemed to like Lady Mary."

"Lady Mary's not exactly a beauty," he said. "Actually, she puts me in mind of my first wife." Maitland paused to consider it a moment before seeming to experience an epiphany. "I wondered why Lady Mary seemed so familiar, as if I'd met her before! She and my wife might have been cousins, they're so alike."

"Perhaps you should tell Lady Smallpeace you suspect Mrs. Maitland was related to her," Sophie suggested jokingly, though she felt a little uncomfortable discussing his deceased wife. "You'd be sure to win her favor if you'd had the wit to marry one of her near relations."

"I wouldn't have the audacity."

"To marry into her family or to tell her so?" Sophie asked.

"Either," Mr. Maitland replied.

Cecilia was left in the box with the two least attractive gentlemen of the group, her mother, some children, and their nursery maid. She could not help but feel that her come-out, which had seemed such an exciting prospect a few months ago, had utterly failed to live up to her expectations.

She was beginning to think she needed to revise her thoughts on love and marriage. Perhaps she had let her mother influence her too much and her ideas of the perfect match *were* too wrapped up in the person's pedigree and material assets, as Sophie had said. Cecilia had come to realize that she'd approached her come-out as a competition and that she had wanted to be the one who carried home the biggest marital prize. But she now saw that she'd been very naïve. In her girlish imaginings on the subject she'd assumed that a wealthy man with an illustrious title would also be someone automatically worthy of love and respect, and that it would be no hardship to grant that to him. But through her association with Lady Smallpeace and Lord Courtney, she had come to realize that titles and bloodlines were no guarantee of true gentility and nobility of spirit.

And she missed Mr. Hartwell. She did still see him from time to time, but it seemed as if he'd cooled in his attentions to her. Last night, for instance, he'd only asked to stand up with her once, and during their dance he had rarely smiled. And he hadn't been to call in three days, though she had grown accustomed to finding him in her drawing room practically every day. When she thought of how unfailingly helpful he had always been and of the many kindnesses he'd performed for her and her family, she began to feel ashamed of having viewed such offerings so lightly and callously. Only now that they were withdrawn could she value such acts, as well as the man who had performed them, at their true worth.

At that very moment, Cecilia, who was gazing idly out at the park, saw Mr. Hartwell walking down a gravel path toward her and thought at first he was an apparition generated by her longings for him. She blinked, but when she opened her eyes he was still there, smiling shyly and fondly.

But not at her. He had a lady on each arm: Mrs. Woodford and her granddaughter Emily. And it was at Emily Woodford he was smiling.

As if Mr. Hartwell felt the weight of Cecilia's gaze, he looked directly at her and saw her watching him. Upon seeing Cecilia, his fair countenance flushed red, but then he nodded and smiled in an attempt to appear nonchalant. He said something to Miss Woodford, who then looked in Cecilia's direction and began smiling and waving at her, the conniving jade. But Cecilia quickly banished that thought, as she knew in her heart of hearts that Emily Woodford was a very estimable young woman, and obviously much more discerning than she was.

Mr. Hartwell and the Woodford ladies stopped at the box to greet those seated inside. Cecilia's mother was also surprised to see Mr. Hartwell with Miss Woodford and glanced quickly at Cecilia to gauge her reaction. Cecilia tried to appear unaffected by her former suitor's appearance with another woman but wondered if by acting as if she did not care she gave herself away even more, and so became quite vivacious and talkative. She explained that Sophie, Mr. Maitland, and the Beswicks had gone into the

Labyrinth and, forgetting that Miss Woodford knew Bath far better than she did, encouraged her to try it. She was afraid she saw a trace of pity in Emily Woodford's expression as she said, "I have visited it in the past and enjoyed it very much." Then Miss Woodford turned and looked coyly at Mr. Hartwell and said, "But perhaps, Mr. Hartwell, you would like to venture inside?"

Instead of replying, Mr. Hartwell looked over at Cecilia, who met his gaze, her aloof façade slipping for a moment and her conflicted feelings plainly displayed on her face. His expression softened a little, but then Lord Courtney chose that inauspicious moment to make his presence known by sneezing three times in rapid succession and then saying, "I beg your pardon. Something is causing a ticklish sensation in my nose. Probably all of this deuced vegetation."

After this Mr. Hartwell and his party took their leave, Miss Woodford asking Cecilia to please tell Sophie she would call on her soon.

Mrs. Foster turned to speak to her daughter after the others had left but, seeing the frozen smile on Cecilia's face, said nothing. Later, as she watched Cecilia and her noble suitor sitting in an awkward and uncomfortable silence, broken only by his fatuous and nonsensical remarks, Mrs. Foster, too, came to an unwelcome realization.

Sophie didn't remember the walk to the center of the Labyrinth being so long and wondered if it was because they were forced to slow their pace to accommodate Mrs. Beswick.

Charles was becoming frustrated, and Sophie could not blame him, though she thought it was most likely Priscilla's slippers that were causing the problem, and not Priscilla.

"Priscilla, *must* you walk so slow?" Sophie overheard Charles asking his wife, in the tone of a man who had endured enough.

"*I* am walking at a ladylike pace; it is *you* who are walking too fast."

"Miss Lattimore's ladylike pace doesn't seem to be as snail-like as yours," Charles said, and Sophie was disconcerted to find herself a bone of contention between the couple. They always seemed to be bickering. She did not understand how they had ever ceased arguing long enough to fall in love and marry.

Mr. Maitland stopped walking and turned back to face the couple. "When a lady presents such a vision of loveliness as your wife, Mr. Beswick, a man is happy to have the opportunity to contemplate it and doesn't complain that he is given the leisure to do so." He punctuated this piece of pretentiousness by bowing to Priscilla.

Sophie did not feel as if Charles Beswick appreciated this remark, and she found it somewhat annoying as well. So she was not as gravely disappointed as she expected she should have been when Charles Beswick said: "Fine, then. *You* walk with her." He left Priscilla's side and walked over to Sophie, offering her his arm. "Miss Lattimore?"

Sophie took his arm without remark, and Mr. Maitland, though he looked regretfully at Sophie, stretched out his arm for Priscilla to take.

Mr. Beswick started walking briskly, and Sophie matched her step to his. Contrary to what Priscilla had said earlier about it being too warm for a walk, Sophie had been somewhat chilled, as the day was overcast and the sun hidden behind a cloud. So she found the increased activity warming and rather exhilarating. But after a few minutes Charles slowed and turned to her with a frown. "I suppose I should beg your pardon, Miss Lattimore. You probably would have preferred to walk with Mr. Maitland."

"I have no complaints," Sophie said.

"That is kind of you to say, but I am aware that I'm behaving childishly." Sophie did not reply, and after a moment, he continued. "You must wonder why it is that Priscilla and I . . . You see, Miss Lattimore, I've known Priscilla since we were both children. I was a few years older and she was 'just' a girl, so obviously I had no time for her." His frown disappeared, transformed into a reminiscent, fond smile. "But when I came home from school she literally forced herself into my presence. She rode faster, ran further . . ." He stopped to shake his head in disbelief. "You should have seen her on the back of a horse, Miss Lattimore, wearing an old riding habit, her hair streaming wildly out from under her bonnet. She was far more beautiful to me than the night I saw her in London in her expensive ball gown, a dozen fops at her feet."

Sophie was quite surprised by the picture of Priscilla he'd just painted. Sophie would have never guessed Priscilla to be interested in any kind of physical activity. If this was whom Charles had thought he'd married, was it any wonder he was disappointed by the dainty fashion plate who had taken her place?

"I am aware you advocated for our match, Miss Lattimore, and I was very grateful to you at the time, as I loved Priscilla most sincerely and had despaired at the thought of losing her. But," he said, his expression becoming bleak again, "is it possible I have lost her already? Where is the girl I fell in love with? She no longer cares for the things we once enjoyed doing together, but only wants to talk about frills and furbelows, beaux and society gossip, and expects constant compliments on her appearance. I care naught for any of those things. It's enough to drive a man to drink!"

"It is indeed, Mr. Beswick," Sophie said sympathetically, as she genuinely felt sorry for him. "I was not aware that Priscilla's personality had changed so drastically. But the girl you fell in love with is still there somewhere, I'm sure," she said, a little mendaciously, as she was sure of no such thing.

Charles Beswick stopped walking abruptly and turned and grabbed Sophie's hand. "Could you help us repair our relationship, Miss Lattimore? Priscilla tells me you have a talent for such things."

Sophie reflected on the fact that no one could have ever been punished for an act of benevolent interference more than she had. And yet she had obviously still not learned her lesson, because she found herself assuring Mr. Beswick she would do her best to help him and Priscilla with their

marriage. She, an unmarried spinster, who could not resolve her own relationship dilemma.

Sophie and Charles Beswick reached the swing long before
the other couple, but since there were a lady and gentleman in the process of using it, Sophie reasoned they would
have had to wait anyway and stifled any impatience she
might have felt. Charles Beswick, too, did not appear to be
worried by his wife's extended absence with another gentleman, but seemed more interested in studying the me-
chanics of the swing.

Merlin's swing was housed in a gazebo-like structure
that had a roof but was open on the sides. The compart-
ment where the participants sat was boat-shaped, had two
bench seats at each end, and was suspended by ropes from
the ceiling. There was also a rope that hung above each
bench seat, and by pulling it a rider could propel the swing
from side to side.

The attendant was willing to hurry the other couple
along (apparently they had already been on the swing for
some time), but Sophie explained to him that they were
waiting for their friends, so he allowed the couple to continue swinging until they'd had their fill. It was just after
they'd finished that Priscilla and Mr. Maitland arrived.

"Finally!" Charles pronounced irritably, but after a warning glance from Sophie he managed to swallow his ire. "You
two arrived just in time," he said, in a much milder tone.

The attendant helped them into the swing, providing some instruction as he did so, though Charles Beswick obviously felt he did not require it. Indeed, he was quite eager to get started, and Priscilla had barely taken her seat before he was already giving his rope a pull.

"Eek!" Priscilla screeched, grabbing her husband's arm.

Mr. Maitland and Sophie had settled beside each other on their bench seat opposite the Beswicks, but Sophie was not quite ready to be catapulted into motion, either, as she was in the midst of trying to figure out how to arrange her skirts so that they would not fly up and expose anything unmentionable to passersby. When the swing began to move, Mr. Maitland steadied Sophie with a hand around her waist, but before she had time to become too self-conscious he removed his hand to grab the rope and pull.

Priscilla had regained her balance but was still holding on to Charles as tightly as she could. He did not appear to mind but smiled affectionately at her before giving the rope another mighty tug.

Sophie was concerned the men were going to launch them into space, as there seemed to be some contest between them over who could propel the swing the furthest. As she was not married to Mr. Maitland, she did not feel comfortable grabbing on to him as Priscilla was doing with *her* husband, so she instead had one hand on the side of the boat and grasped the underside of the bench with the other. She felt she would have enjoyed the experience far more if she and Priscilla had been the ones in charge of the rope-pulling. Although for once Priscilla was not complaining about her husband's behavior but seemed to be enjoying the wild ride, laughing and squealing and squeezing her husband's muscular arm. Sophie began to see a semblance of the girl Priscilla had been before, and from the fond glances Charles was casting at her, it appeared he was seeing the same.

It was Sophie who felt the urge to complain, and she may have done so if the attendant hadn't shouted a warning to the two men not to pull the ropes so hard.

Once they were swinging at a gentler pace and were not in imminent danger of being hurled from the contraption, Mr. Maitland turned to speak to Sophie. "You are welcome to hold on to my arm."

Sophie had often taken Mr. Maitland's arm when they walked together, but it seemed rather forward of her to do so while he was engaged in activity that caused his muscles to tense, something that Sophie could feel through the fabric of his coat and caused her to become much warmer than she had during her brisk walk with Mr. Beswick. She was feeling extremely ill at ease, and felt even more so when she looked across at the Beswicks, who were staring at each other heatedly as if they were about to resume their interrupted honeymoon.

But then Charles, while pulling on the rope, swiped the side of Priscilla's head and dislodged her hat, just before a rush of wind swept it from her head.

"Oh, no!" Priscilla cried, standing up in the swing and looking as if she were going to leap out in pursuit of her hat, which had landed on the ground a few feet away. Charles stopped her before she could do so, pulling her down beside him and laughing and saying, "It's just a hat, Priscilla. I'll buy you another."

"Just a hat! *Just a hat!*" Priscilla repeated in disbelief. "Men have written *odes* to that hat! One compared it to the nimbus of a goddess!"

Before Charles could respond, the attendant had run over to the headgear and snatched it up, slapping it against his thigh in an attempt to remove any dirt it may have acquired. They all watched as an egret feather floated sadly to the ground.

"No harm done," the attendant said. "It'll be waiting for you when you've finished the ride."

But that incident effectively *did* finish the ride, as even Mr. Maitland couldn't smooth things over when Charles failed to show the proper remorse (or any at all) for his part in destroying Priscilla's favorite *chapeau*. The newlyweds, who had been enraptured with each other only moments before, were now barely speaking to each other, and their mood infected Sophie and Mr. Maitland as well, as it halted any romantic overtures on his part and he and Sophie began exchanging polite platitudes in an attempt to pretend nothing untoward was occurring.

11

The excursion that Sophie had thought would clarify her conflicted feelings failed miserably in that regard, but apparently had the opposite effect on Cecilia, who came away from Sydney Gardens determined that she would never marry Lord Courtney and convinced that her true love was Mr. Hartwell, whom she had unfortunately lost to another.

Sophie valiantly overcame any desire to tell her "I told you so," and instead listened very sympathetically to Cecilia's laments. Sophie was not only sad for her cousin but sorry for herself as well, because she did not see how she could continue her friendship with Emily Woodford, the woman who had stolen the affections of the man her cousin loved. Of course Sophie knew Emily was blameless; she had been present when the couple had first met and recognized that Emily's attraction toward Mr. Hartwell was genuine, and Cecilia had been very publicly encouraging a different man's attentions. Still, she realized it would pain Cecilia to be forced into association with the couple through Sophie's friendship with Emily, and Sophie knew her first loyalty lay with Cecilia.

Sophie could remember very well how it had felt at eighteen to have the man you admire reject you in favor of another, and although Cecilia had only her own stupidity to blame for her loss of Mr. Hartwell's affection, Sophie had no doubt that made it sting even more bitterly.

Mrs. Foster had not discussed the matter with her daughter, Cecilia's tearful revelations having taken place in the privacy of Sophie's bedchamber once they'd returned from the gardens, but Mrs. Foster did announce over dinner that they must all be tired from their excursion and that they would spend a rare evening at home rather than attend the assembly rooms.

Sophie felt as if this was just delaying the inevitable meeting between all parties involved, but she appreciated that Aunt Foster seemed to be cognizant of Cecilia's distress and was trying to help. And when later she heard her aunt knock on Cecilia's door and ask to speak to her, Sophie desperately hoped her solution wasn't to pressure her daughter into making a disastrous match with Lord Courtney.

But the next morning at breakfast Sophie found her worries were unfounded. She and Mrs. Foster were alone, Cecilia not having come down, when Mrs. Foster explained that she now recognized her folly in encouraging Cecilia to reject Mr. Hartwell's suit in favor of Lord Courtney's.

"It is a difficult thing for me to admit," Mrs. Foster told Sophie as she toyed with the food on her plate, "but I have failed my daughter."

Sophie wished she could deny this claim, as Aunt Foster looked ten years older that morning in the bright light streaming through the window, the dark shadows under her eyes harshly illuminated. But Sophie knew any protestations she made would be hollow and unconvincing, so she remained silent. And after a moment Mrs. Foster began telling Sophie things she had never confided in another living soul.

"I had a cousin my own age whom I was raised with; we made our come-out together. But she was my superior in every way; looks, manner, charm. I was completely overshadowed by her, and when she made a brilliant match to a wealthy earl, I felt my failure even more acutely. I was far from a success. So awkward and shy and plain, or at least I felt that way in comparison to my cousin. Mr. Foster was the only gentleman to make me an offer, and so I accepted him.

"Poor man," Mrs. Foster said with a self-mocking smile, "he did not win much of a prize. Instead of appreciating that I had a husband who treated me with kindness and gave me a beautiful daughter, I instead dwelled upon what I thought I had missed out on: a title and a respected position in society. I thought my marriage confirmation of what I knew to be true of myself: I was lesser, unworthy, a failure."

"Was your cousin happy in her marriage?" Sophie asked.

Mrs. Foster shrugged. "I do not know. She did not complain, at any rate, even though the earl was widely reputed to be a philanderer. She seemed to enjoy her social status, but she didn't have long to do so. She died in childbirth just over a year later."

"I am so sorry."

"Yes, it was very sad. Perhaps if she'd lived longer I'd have come to recognize how misguided my thinking was, but instead I became stuck in that view, and continued to believe my cousin had achieved the pinnacle of success for a female and that I was an utter failure. And then when Cecilia grew into such a handsome young lady, so charming and self-assured, I began to think *she* was my opportunity for redemption, that her success would mitigate my deficiencies."

"Aunt Foster, you are too hard on yourself—" Sophie began, but her aunt waved her to silence.

"Don't worry. I have come to realize, far too late, that my judgment was flawed. And that Mr. Foster *was* the superior marital prize, little though I recognized it at the time. But I encouraged Cecilia to have the same warped view of marriage that I had, and I can see it's made her very miserable indeed."

Sophie couldn't deny this, and the two sat in silence for a few minutes, before Mrs. Foster ventured, "Perhaps it's not too late for her and Mr. Hartwell."

"It may not be," Sophie agreed. "One excursion in the park with Emily Woodford does not a marriage make. But I would do nothing to encourage Cecilia's hopes in that regard."

"No, of course not, but perhaps *you* could do something to assist your cousin? Something similar to what you did for Lucy Barrett and Lord Fitzwalter?"

And Sophie had cause to regret, yet again, that she had ever written that letter.

Sophie was thankful when Priscilla Beswick called later that morning, as she was able to convince Priscilla to accompany her to the Pump Room. Since Cecilia and Mrs. Foster were not at all eager to face Lady Smallpeace and Lord Courtney, they were eschewing their usual social appearances for the time being, and Sophie, too, would have been forced to remain at home. So she found herself greeting Priscilla warmly, even though the last time she'd seen her had been at the disastrous excursion to Sydney Gardens.

Which was what Priscilla wanted to discuss as they walked to the Pump Room together. "I realize I may have overreacted a trifle to the destruction of my hat, but Charles is so unsympathetic, there is no bearing it! Mr. Maitland is *far* more understanding. Do you mean to have him?"

Sophie, who had only been listening with half an ear to Priscilla's complaints about her husband (and her ruined hat), was jolted to attention by this abrupt question. "What?"

"I thought when I first arrived in Bath it was Sir Edmund whom you admired, and he would no doubt be the more brilliant match, but then Mr. Maitland is so"—here Priscilla paused before finally finding the word she was searching for and uttering it in a breathy sigh—"*simpatico*. He's even more agreeable than Lord Fitzwalter. I honestly wonder if I'd met him before I knew Charles . . ." Priscilla shrugged without finishing her sentence. "But, then again, if I hadn't known Charles I would have likely married Fitzwalter."

Sophie was relieved that Priscilla seemed to forget her question regarding Sophie's intentions as she became involved in a complicated analysis of her own current and former gentlemen admirers. She required little more than a nod of agreement and a sympathetic murmur, which allowed Sophie to ponder her own tangled affairs, and her cousin's. Still, Sophie hadn't forgotten she'd offered to help the Beswicks as well, and she did try, interrupting Priscilla's musings to ask: "Priscilla, is it true that you were far more interested in physical pursuits when Mr. Beswick first began courting you? Had you thought that he might enjoy spending time with you in some of those activities far more than balls and morning calls?"

"I did enjoy those things when I was younger, but Charles has to have realized that when I put my hair up I was finished with all of that. I learned when I went to London that my youthful behavior, while permissible before I'd made my come-out, was completely unsuitable for a lady of quality. Why, you are not even permitted to gallop in Hyde Park!

Charles certainly cannot expect a woman who has been the toast of London to gad about like a wild schoolgirl."

Before Sophie could find a way to contradict this assertion, she and Priscilla had reached the entrance to the Pump Room and been hailed by one of Priscilla's many admirers, and any private conversation between them was perforce concluded.

Sophie had no clear idea how to help Cecilia other than to somehow hint to Mr. Hartwell that Cecilia had decided not to entertain Lord Courtney's suit any longer, since it seemed to Sophie this must be why he had ceased his attentions to her. Therefore, when Sophie entered the Pump Room she was so intent on finding Mr. Hartwell that when instead she immediately encountered Sir Edmund, she was completely taken aback and thrown into total confusion.

"Miss Lattimore, how do you do?" he asked, and she curtsied in response.

"Quite well, I thank you," she replied, but she blushed as she said it and looked so strange that Sir Edmund thought the opposite.

"Are you sure you are not suffering from the heat? Would you take my arm?" he said, concerned.

"No, no, I am fine," she said, but then, seizing upon the excuse he offered, Sophie continued, "though Mrs. Beswick and I did have rather a long walk, so perhaps I am a trifle overheated." She turned to Priscilla for confirmation of this remark but found that she was engaged in her own conversation with Mr. Andrews. Sophie realized that this was probably for the best, because Priscilla was so unpredictable that she was as likely to contradict Sophie's statement as she was to confirm it.

"It is rather crowded here. Perhaps we could walk closer to the window," Sir Edmund said.

Sophie took his arm, and they walked to a bench by a window, where she sat down, mentally berating herself for her lack of composure. But it had been a few days since she'd seen Sir Edmund, and she had neglected to prepare herself for a meeting with him. She realized suddenly that, while she also felt uneasy and confused in Mr. Maitland's presence, this exhilaration she was feeling was caused by Sir Edmund alone. But should she indulge these feelings? What if they were not reciprocated? Wouldn't Mr. Maitland be the safer choice?

But these were not thoughts she could ponder at the present moment, so she took some deep breaths in an attempt to regain her sangfroid.

"How are you feeling?" Sir Edmund asked.

"I am fine. But I do thank you, it is far more pleasant in this corner of the room."

"It is indeed," said Sir Edmund with a smile that had a touch of the flirtatious in it, and Sophie was reminded of when she offered to tutor him in the skill and blushed again at her foolishness.

There was silence for a moment, as Sophie shyly stared

down at her hands and Sir Edmund studied her. And then Sir Edmund cleared his throat before saying, "I am glad we have this opportunity to be private. I have something I want to ask you."

Sophie's eyes flew to his, but he immediately rushed into further speech, as if aware that such a beginning could portend more than he'd intended. "That is, I should have said I wished to offer you an invitation."

Sophie nodded encouragingly. She was bemused by how awkward and diffident Sir Edmund could become at times. He seemed even more shy and uncomfortable with the opposite sex than she was! And then at other times he seemed a practiced flirt, as she had reason to know.

"I wondered if you—and your aunt and cousin, of course—would care to spend a day at my estate, Newbrooke. It is no more than an hour by carriage from Bath, and I could arrange transportation. And my housekeeper Mrs. Cooper could make arrangements for tea and the like."

He had barely finished his sentence before Sophie was rushing into a pleased acceptance. "Yes! That would be lovely, thank you! I can think of nothing I'd like more."

"It is I who would be honored by your visit," Sir Edmund said, smiling at her excitement. "Is there someone else you would like me to invite? Your particular friend Miss Woodford, for example?"

"No!" Sophie said, a little too vehemently, and Sir Edmund raised one eyebrow in surprise. "No, thank you, not Miss Woodford. But do you think, perhaps—would you invite Mr. Hartwell?" Sophie asked. "And also, if it's not asking too much, the Beswicks?"

Sir Edmund did not reply for a moment and then began to chuckle. "Miss Lattimore, have you decided to take up matchmaking again, after protesting vigorously that people should be allowed to manage their own affairs and that you could not, would not, interfere?"

Sophie looked about her, to be sure no one had heard Sir Edmund. "Please, Sir Edmund, lower your voice. It is not matchmaking, precisely, but rather an attempt to rectify the problems caused by previous matchmaking efforts, both mine and others'."

"I see," Sir Edmund said, but he appeared to be making an effort to restrain a smile. "If Beswick and Hartwell are coming then I suppose I need to arrange for more than tea and biscuits. Do you ride, Miss Lattimore?"

"I do, though I haven't done so in years."

"What about the other ladies? Somehow I cannot picture Mrs. Beswick on horseback, galloping *ventre à terre* and putting her coiffure at danger of becoming disarranged."

"Oh, you would be surprised. I am told she is quite the horsewoman. But perhaps you should just plan on rides for the gentlemen."

Their tête-à-tête was interrupted at that point by the very gentleman Sophie had been searching for earlier. Mr. Hartwell greeted them both and then turned to address Sophie, looking self-conscious as he did so. "I do not see your aunt and cousin with you. I trust they are both in good health?"

Sophie rose from the bench in order to converse more easily with Mr. Hartwell, as Sir Edmund had been standing slightly bent toward her with his arm resting against the wall, partially obscuring her from view.

"They are not ill, but Cecilia is suffering from a slight depression of spirits," she said, and hoped that her cousin would never discover she had told Mr. Hartwell so.

"I am sorry to hear it," Mr. Hartwell said, but he looked more confused than sorry, as if he could not decide what significance this remark might have, if any. "Please give her my regards. Or, no, well, yes, I suppose you can pass on my greetings. If you don't think it would dampen her spirits further," Mr. Hartwell said, and once again looked as if he was unsure whether to hope for or against such an eventuality.

"I think it would raise her spirits tremendously that you thought kindly of her, or indeed, that she was in your thoughts at all," Sophie said, and tried to ignore Sir Edmund's slight cough, which she felt was produced on purpose to tease her.

"I'm sure she's more concerned with Lord Courtney's opinion of her than mine," Mr. Hartwell said, and his open, placid countenance assumed the most bitter expression it could, which made him look a little like a grumpy young cherub.

Sophie had hoped for such an opening, and gratefully

took it. "May I tell you something in confidence, Mr. Hartwell?" She turned briefly to Sir Edmund. "I am sure I can trust Sir Edmund as a gentleman not to repeat anything I might say." Sir Edmund bowed very gravely, though Sophie thought she saw an inappropriate twinkle in his eye. Ignoring him, she stepped closer to Mr. Hartwell and lowered her voice. "It appears that my aunt Foster has been promoting a match between my cousin and . . . someone I shall not name, though I believe you may have just mentioned him." Sophie raised her eyebrows significantly as she said this, and Mr. Hartwell nodded his understanding. "And Cecilia is such a dutiful daughter that she tried to accede to her mother's wishes, but upon closer acquaintance with this unnamed gentleman, found that nothing could induce her to enter into a binding commitment with him. And now she is quite inconsolable at the thought of disappointing her mother. I think you can understand what has caused her depression of spirits, can you not, Mr. Hartwell? And I hope you shall remain her friend."

"But of course! Poor Cecil—er—Miss Foster; I will do everything in my power to cheer her."

"I am so relieved to hear that! I was sure we could rely upon you, Mr. Hartwell," Sophie said admiringly, and Mr. Hartwell immediately colored up. Sophie refused to look at Sir Edmund, afraid that he would cause her to lose her composure with a teasing glance. So she was surprised and grateful when he took charge of the conversation at that point, inviting Mr. Hartwell to join in the visit to his estate, which was then tentatively scheduled for a week hence.

Once their plans were made, Mr. Hartwell soon took his leave of them both, and Sophie finally ventured to peep up at Sir Edmund, her eyebrows raised as if asking a question. He met her gaze with a smile, and then clapped lightly. "Brava! What a masterful performance," he said. "I am in awe. And also in fear, as every unmarried gentleman in your vicinity should be."

"Nonsense," Sophie said, embarrassed. "Everything I said was true, though I may have painted Aunt Foster's behavior as worse than it actually was."

"But you had to, in order to stir the gentleman's chivalrous instincts. And I'm certain any mother would be more than willing to sacrifice her reputation if it was done in such a cause," Sir Edmund replied. "Why was all of this necessary, by the way? I had assumed Hartwell's heart to already be firmly in your cousin's possession. Had he deserted her because of her folly in encouraging that nincompoop Courtney?"

"Yes, and had begun to look elsewhere."

"That must have brought Miss Foster to her senses rather quickly. He should have done that weeks ago," Sir Edmund said.

"Why, Sir Edmund, you appear to be quite skilled at the management of affairs of the heart yourself," Sophie congratulated him.

"Oh, no, I am not skilled in the least at maneuvering such matters. I bow to your superior knowledge. Indeed, I encourage you to exercise your talents in my behalf. My heart is yours to manage," he said, and this time he did not quickly retract his statement, or look away in embarrassment, but stared meaningfully at her. And when Priscilla Beswick approached, saying that she had been looking for Sophie everywhere, and what did she mean by hiding away in this corner with Sir Edmund, Sophie had the greatest difficulty tearing herself away from Sir Edmund's mesmerizing gaze.

12

When Sophie returned home from the Pump Room, she found that Cecilia had come down with a cold (perhaps brought on by the lowness of her spirits), which gave the ladies an excellent excuse to offer for not receiving callers or going out. Thankfully it was not a serious illness, and it appeared as if she would be fully recovered by the time they were to visit Sir Edmund's estate. When Cecilia learned that Mr. Hartwell would be accompanying them, she began looking forward to the excursion nearly as much as Sophie was. Sophie, who felt she now knew which of her suitors she preferred and had some reason to believe he might feel likewise, obviously could not reveal her partiality for *him* before he confessed his for *her*, and hoped that this might occur during their visit to Sir Edmund's estate. So she was as intent on avoiding Mr. Maitland as Cecilia was Lord Courtney.

Mr. Hartwell had sent Cecilia flowers, which she kept at her bedside table, and when they began to droop, she selected one to carefully press between the pages of her diary. (Sophie noticed that a bouquet from Lord Courtney had been left in a dark corner of the drawing room, to wilt unseen and unlamented.)

Sophie had not been neglected by her erstwhile suitor, either, as Mr. Maitland had sent her a poem he had found that had been written by a woman poetess of the previous century, Mary Leapor, titled "Advice to Sophronia." Sophie was very touched upon receiving it, and even felt guilty that she could not reciprocate Mr. Maitland's affection. That is, until she read the poem, something she felt sure Mr. Maitland must not have taken the time to do.

"When youth and charms have ta'en their wanton flight," it began, "And transient beauty bids the fair good-night; When once her sparkling eyes shall dimly roll, Then let the matron dress her lofty soul; Quit affectation, partner of her youth, For goodness, prudence, purity and truth."

But the insulting advice to the aged, decrepit, and apparently vain and shallow Sophronia did not stop there. On the contrary, it continued:

> *Time's rugged hand has stroked your visage o'er;*
> *The gay vermilion stains your lip no more.*
> *None can with justice now your shape admire;*
> *The drooping lilies on your breast expire.*

And after more choice descriptions of "shriveled arms" and "once-lovely eyes," it ended with this dreary prophecy:

Ye pitying Fates, this withered damsel save,
And bear her safely to her virgin grave.

At first reading Sophie was surprised and offended, but then she had to laugh at what Mr. Maitland had intended as a grand romantic gesture, and finally decided to save it in *her* diary. After all, it was the first poem she'd ever been given by an admirer. No gentlemen were writing odes to Sophie's attire, as they had Priscilla Beswick's. But neither were they comparing her to cows, so she eventually decided the gift of a poem which contained her name in the title was not necessarily an insult, after all.

Mr. Hartwell, now that he was back in Cecilia's favor and she in his, had happily taken it upon himself to arrange the ladies' transportation to Newbrooke. As the Beswicks had also accepted Sir Edmund's invitation, it was decided that the four ladies would travel by carriage while Misters Beswick and Hartwell would accompany the carriage on horseback.

The first meeting between Cecilia and Mr. Hartwell since their last encounter at Sydney Gardens and Cecilia's realization of her feelings for him was less awkward than it might have been, as there was so much hustle and bustle involved with preparations for the trip that they were able to do no more than exchange greetings, though they did so with a heightened color and an air of consciousness. But of course Priscilla Beswick must be at the center of every activity, and that morning was no different, as she soon was distracting attention away from the timid couple with earnest questions about the length of the trip and if it was possible for her to sit facing forward, as she was inclined toward motion sickness. Charles looked impatient at his wife's queries, and Sophie had to agree that if Priscilla really was the daredevil he'd described, this pretense of delicacy was a little much. But she had come to recognize that Priscilla thought all these little affectations she'd adopted were the appropriate behavior of a leading society lady. In fact, now that Sophie understood Priscilla's thinking, she could even recognize mannerisms Priscilla had copied from some of the more popular London belles. And Priscilla was correct that these tactics usually did result in a greater share of the gentlemen's attention. It was unfortunate, however, that Priscilla's own husband was not a fan of such ploys. Therefore, Sophie did not contradict Priscilla's claims of fragility but quickly offered to sit across from her in the carriage, and Cecilia volunteered the same so that her mother could also face forward, and they were finally on their way.

Once they had left the city proper, the gentlemen were seen passing the carriage, riding vigorously and with obvious enjoyment. They had good reason to be pleased, as the weather had cooperated with their excursion, and though there were a few puffy white clouds, the sky was of an astonishingly deep shade of blue.

"Mr. Hartwell has a good seat," Priscilla commented suddenly as the ladies watched the gentlemen ride by, and Cecilia blushed and again looked self-conscious. "But I wonder why *he* is escorting you. I thought you meant to have Lord Courtney," she said to Cecilia, to the consternation of all of the ladies, who would have preferred such a remark to have remained unspoken.

"Well, I—I . . ." Cecilia stuttered, and looked to Sophie for assistance.

"Priscilla, you should know better than anyone that nothing is certain until the banns are called," Sophie said.

Priscilla blinked at Sophie as she attempted to make sense of her words, finally coming up with an interpretation Sophie had not intended. "Oh, Lord," Priscilla replied. "Did you write another one of your letters?"

There was a momentary silence following Priscilla's remark, and then Sophie began to laugh. Cecilia was soon giggling as well, and even Mrs. Foster's frown was replaced by a small smile. After this lighthearted beginning to their trip, Mrs. Foster diverted the conversation away from any further discussion of men or marriage by asking Priscilla about her home in Devon, and the foursome were soon chattering away quite happily. So enjoyable and engrossing was the conversation that when the castellated gatehouse came into view, the women were shocked that they'd arrived at Newbrooke so quickly, and Sophie, at least, was upset that she hadn't paid more attention to her surroundings, as she had a particular interest in Sir Edmund's home that went deeper than that of the others.

As the carriage passed through the gate and onto Sir Edmund's property, Sophie leaned forward for a better view and promptly collided with Priscilla, who was doing the same. But for once Priscilla deferred to Sophie, drawing back with a mischievous smile and gesturing for Sophie to look out the carriage window. Sophie smiled her thanks and leaned forward again, but soon felt Priscilla's hand on her shoulder and her breath against her cheek, and before too long was listening to her admiring commentary about the grandeur of Sir Edmund's estate.

It *was* a grand sight. The brook from which the estate derived its name babbled happily on one side of the drive, with a Palladian bridge coming into view after they'd rounded a bend in the road, while a Greek folly could be seen sitting serenely at the top of a hill once they'd gone around another. Sophie knew that Sir Edmund was considered a "catch" and so had assumed he was wealthy, but she was a little taken aback all the same. She began to wonder if she had imagined he'd displayed a preference for her company, and that any romance was all in her head. Could she be acting as she had when she was eighteen, when she'd been so sure of Mr. Maitland's regard and thought him on the verge of a marriage proposal? Why would Sir Edmund Winslow of Newbrooke consider Miss Sophronia Lattimore of nowhere and nothing a worthy recipient of his hand? Such a thing defied explanation.

She was a little relieved upon finally approaching the house. It was a lovely manor house, stately and elegant, and its honey-colored limestone gleamed in the late-morning light, but it looked to be no more than a hundred years old and was not at all the gargantuan Tudor or Elizabethan mansion she had been expecting. However, it was still a great deal more elegant than she was, and she tried to gather her tattered bits of self-esteem, telling herself she was as worthy of love and happiness as any person, that such things had nothing at all to do with family connections, wealth, or physical appearance. Yet just then her gaze chanced to fall upon Priscilla Beswick, who had not one russet-colored hair out of place and whose French carriage dress exuded elegance, and Sophie could not help thinking she should have at least purchased a new pair of gloves for this occasion.

Before she had time to dwell any further on her defects, the door was opened and she was being helped down from the carriage. She and the ladies were directed up the front stairs into the vestibule and from there into the drawing room, where the gentlemen were waiting for them.

Sir Edmund turned at their entrance, and Sophie was relieved to see he scanned all the ladies' faces, even Priscilla Beswick's, without pausing until his gaze fell upon her, at which time his expression transformed into a tender smile.

"You have arrived at last! I am so happy to welcome you—welcome you all—to Newbrooke," he said, bowing to the four ladies, but Sophie didn't think she was deluding herself this time in believing that he was speaking most particularly to her.

After they had partaken of a cold collation in the dining room, Sir Edmund announced that his housekeeper would show the ladies the house while he took the gentlemen on a riding tour of the grounds. Mr. Beswick was quick to agree to this plan, but Mr. Hartwell hesitated, casting a quick glance at Cecilia.

"We have been on horseback all morning, and I would like to see the interior of the house. I'm very interested in"—he waved his hand about vaguely, searching for the correct word—"home décor. You know, draperies, sofas, rugs, and all that. I'm thinking of redecorating soon myself."

"I think, Charles, that you should come as well," Priscilla told her husband. "Birch House is desperately in need of refurbishing. It obviously could never be as grand as *this*, but in its current state it looks positively shabby."

"My dear, I had no idea you were at all interested in such matters. How positively wifely of you. I find myself very eager to join this tour," Charles said, extending his arm to his wife.

The housekeeper, seeing that the lord of the manor was to be present after all, begged that he give the tour in her stead, as his knowledge was bound to exceed hers.

"Nonsense; I am sure the opposite is true. Mrs. Cooper is much more skilled at giving tours than I, and you would likely learn a good deal more from her than from me," Sir Edmund told the others. "However, I will assume the role this once and trust that my audience will exercise a great deal of forbearance," he concluded, as he could see his housekeeper was nervous at the thought of giving the tour in his company.

Sophie was pleased at his kind treatment of this member of his staff and thought that his oversight of Newbrooke in general appeared to be a benevolent one. Of course, she realized she'd been there scarcely two hours and could not really know the true state of affairs, but there was an air of ease and comfort among the servants she'd seen thus far, and she'd visited grand estates where the opposite was true and the discontent of the staff could be sensed immediately, casting a dark shadow over any splendor of well-designed architecture or gilded furnishings.

The tour began in the Blue Drawing Room, where they had all first met, but in the excitement of greetings, Sophie had failed to fully assimilate her surroundings. She was still having a difficult time taking it all in, especially the beautiful plasterwork that decorated the walls and the ceiling. She felt sure she was going to get a crick in her neck from looking upward, but it was such a work of beauty and there was so much to see, she could not bring herself to look away.

Sophie was correct in her supposition that the present house was not centuries old, but that was only because, as Sir Edmund explained during the tour, his great-great-grandfather had razed the Tudor mansion that had once been there and commissioned Sir John Vanbrugh to build a new one in its place. The construction of the present house was completed almost a hundred years ago in 1720, but then Sir Edmund's grandfather, not content with *his* grandfather's efforts, had begun a renovation in the 1760s and had commissioned Robert Adam to redesign the interiors.

"And do you, Sir Edmund, intend on continuing the pattern of every second generation?" Charles Beswick asked him.

Sir Edmund looked surprised for a moment, as if he hadn't recognized that a pattern had developed and that it was up to him whether it would be continued or broken. Finally, he smiled and shook his head. "I don't think I could improve upon my grandfather's efforts, and it would be a desecration to undo all of this," he said, gesturing around him at the friezes, cornices, and works of art that were on display. Looking more closely at the furnishings that Sir Edmund had told them were largely designed by Chippendale, Sophie noticed that they, too, fit the overall neoclassical theme, and she agreed with Sir Edmund that he should not alter such a masterpiece. But she once again began thinking that her modest person had no place in such a vision of elegance and, feeling overwhelmed, followed the group into the next room in silence, even though Sir Edmund had looked at her questioningly, as if expecting her to comment.

The tour of Newbrooke's interior finished at the library at the back of the house, which exited onto a terrace overlooking parterre gardens, so the group had quite naturally continued their explorations by stepping out the French doors and into the grounds. While still on the terrace, Sir Edmund pointed out various features that could be seen in the distance, including a "secret" walled garden, the dairy, and the orangery, but after that everyone broke off into pairs, wandering as they saw fit and no longer part of an "official" tour. Mrs. Foster, who had become fatigued by all the walking she'd done already, decided to wait for the younger members of the party inside and was conducted to a comfortable location by Mrs. Cooper.

That left Cecilia and Mr. Hartwell, the Beswicks, and Sophie and Sir Edmund to their own devices. Priscilla, who had wondered aloud whether she should also wait indoors, was finally led along with her husband to examine the stable block, though she was heard to protest that the hem of her petticoat was liable to get dirtied in such an excursion. They were out of earshot before Sophie could hear Charles' reply to his wife's concerns, but she doubted it was sympathetic.

She sighed aloud at the very poor job she had made of this particular match, and Sir Edmund looked at her sympathetically, seemingly able to read her mind. "They do appear to be somewhat ill-suited," he said quietly.

"It is undoubtedly a Divine judgment upon me. I overreached my authority as a mere mortal and now I'm being punished for my vanity and conceit."

Sir Edmund smiled. "I doubt that. You do not appear to me to possess either of those qualities to an excessive degree."

Sophie, thinking back on her feelings of worthlessness

when faced with Sir Edmund's obvious eligibility, couldn't deny that she was not really vain or conceited. That brought to mind the poem Mr. Maitland had given her and she was startled into a gurgle of laughter.

"What is so amusing?" Sir Edmund asked, though he was tempted to laugh, too. It was such a pleasant, infectious, *attractive* sound, he thought to himself, and as he watched Sophie walking slowly through the gravel paths of the gardens, her profile framed here and there by blooms and leaves, not once did he think her out of place or ill-suited to her glorious surroundings. On the contrary, he reflected that she seemed as lovely in her unaffected way as the exquisitely wrought paintings by Gainsborough that graced Newbrooke's walls and the delicately molded Sèvres and Chinese porcelain in its cabinets.

She raised those marvelous gray eyes, now brimming with amusement, up to his, and his breath caught in his chest. "I am just laughing at a poem that Mr. Maitland gave me. I only wish I had it with me so that I could read it to you. 'Advice to Sophronia,' it is called," Sophie said, but wished she could have bitten out her tongue as it was obvious as soon as she mentioned Mr. Maitland that the mood between her and Sir Edmund had changed dramatically. His gaze, which just a moment before had appeared frankly admiring as it played upon her features, had immediately grown distant and cold.

"He wrote it for you? A love poem, no doubt," he said, breaking the awkward silence, though his voice was strained and his attempt to sound lighthearted failed miserably.

"Oh, no, not at all. I would not be laughing or discussing it with you if that were the case. That would be in the worst possible taste. I'm sorry I brought it up at all, as it is inconsiderate of me to ridicule his gift, which I have no doubt was kindly meant, but then I am fairly certain he did not read the poem himself, and he definitely should have. It was written by a lady poet, advising an elderly Sophronia whose beauty had faded past reclaiming to cultivate her inner qualities, as that was all that she had left to her at any rate. *She* had obviously been very vain and conceited, which is why your words put me in mind of the poem. At first I was quite offended that I had been compared to *that* Sophronia, but then it struck me as terribly humorous."

Sophie was relieved to see some of Sir Edmund's stiffness fade at her explanation, but neither did he appear as if he found it funny in the least, and once again she regretted introducing the subject. She desperately tried to think of something to say that would restore their previous harmony. Really, it had been more than harmony; it had almost seemed like affection, even love, and she could kick herself for ruining the moment. However, before she could say anything, Sir Edmund spoke, his thoughts apparently still dwelling upon Mr. Maitland.

"Please forgive me if you think this none of my affair, but I have noticed Mr. Maitland's very obvious partiality for you, and I wondered that you did not accept him when you knew each other before. That is, I had heard you had known each other previously, when you were quite young.

Was that the issue? You felt yourself too young to enter into a lasting bond?"

"No, that was not the reason. I was no younger than most ladies are when they are married. I was eighteen when he—courted me," Sophie said, hesitating over the word.

"That seems quite young to me, but if that was not the reason . . ." Sir Edmund said, his voice trailing off as if he knew that this was an intrusive line of questioning but could not contain himself. However, Sophie knew it was more than idle curiosity that prompted his question, that if he was considering pursuing a relationship with her, this was something he deserved to know. Certainly if Sir Edmund were involved with a young woman to the extent she was involved with Mr. Maitland, she would desire an explanation herself.

Still, she didn't know how to explain without making herself look pathetic and unlovable and so did not comment for a moment while she gathered her thoughts, but continued walking until she saw a bench in an alcove up ahead.

"May we sit there while we talk?" she asked, and he agreed, running his hand over the bench first to ensure there was nothing that could mark her skirts before inviting her to sit.

But when they were both seated Sophie wondered if this was altogether a good idea. There were flowering vines growing over an arched trellis under which the bench was placed, and they had grown so thickly that the two of them were completely hidden from view. Sophie was reminded of the night of the musical concert, when Sir Edmund's nearness had had such an overwhelming effect upon her, and she was experiencing some of the same symptoms at this moment. However, she made a concerted effort to gather her thoughts and finally began to speak, though she found her voice was a little uncertain and she had to clear her throat. "As you mentioned, I was quite young when Mr. Maitland courted me, but I would probably have accepted him had he offered," Sophie said, stretching the truth a bit, as she most definitely would have accepted him. Still, a lady was entitled to *some* secrets. "He showed every indication of making me an offer, but then he proposed to a woman of fortune and married her instead."

"But he seems so enamored of you, I thought it was *you* who had turned *him* down," Sir Edmund said, and it was obvious he was surprised.

"I was given no opportunity to do so, as he never proposed to me," Sophie said.

"Do you intend to do so if he offers for you now that he's free? Because it seems apparent that is his purpose."

Sophie sighed. "It has always been my desire to marry, Sir Edmund, and as you have mentioned in the past, finding a suitable match is not at all an easy matter, especially for a lady like myself who has no large dowry. What if Mr. Maitland is my last opportunity of marrying and having a family?"

"But that is complete nonsense! You are so lovely, Miss

Lattimore—*Sophie*," he said, drawing out her name and speaking it in such a caressing tone that Sophie shivered. "You could surely have any man you desired. And Frederick Maitland, bah!" he said, his tone changing to one of contempt. "I do not deny he has a great deal of superficial charm, but he is not worthy of even a glance from you. Sophie," he said again, his voice urgent now as he reached out and grasped her by the shoulders. "You cannot marry him; promise me you will not."

They were now facing each other in a near-embrace, only inches apart, and they both seemed confused at how they had come to be in such a position. Sophie had almost forgotten what it was that they were discussing, other than that he was asking for a promise from her.

"I promise," she said, though she wasn't entirely sure what she was agreeing to. Sir Edmund also appeared to have lost track of the conversation. He made no response as his eyes darted over her face, finally coming to rest on her lips, while one of his hands drifted up from her shoulder to caress the bare skin at the back of her neck.

Sophie shivered again, wondering how she could be chilled in the middle of summer, and then she ceased to think at all as his lips came down upon hers.

13

⤬⤬

Cecilia and Mr. Hartwell were finding the grounds of Newbrooke delightful as well. As they walked further from the house, Cecilia reflected on the fact that, as many months as Mr. Hartwell had been courting her, they had never once been alone together. Of course, they were not really alone now, as if she looked back she could see Sophie and Sir Edmund walking behind them. She glanced over her shoulder and to her surprise could not see the other couple at all. And then Mr. Hartwell suggested they enter the secret garden that Sir Edmund had pointed out to them.

Cecilia wondered how she should respond—surely the proper thing would be for her to demand to be returned to her chaperone—but when she looked at Mr. Hartwell, she realized there was not a person on earth whom she trusted more than him. Her heart softened at the sight of his dear face, a familiar expression of adoration on it as he looked at her. So she agreed to his suggestion, and he opened the heavy wooden door for her to enter, then shut it behind them.

They walked the small garden in silence, and Cecilia began to wonder why it was he'd wanted to be alone with her if he had nothing to say. But then he finally began speaking. "Miss Foster, I was greatly distressed when your cousin told me how your mother was pressuring you to accept Lord Courtney's suit."

"Sophie told you what?" Cecilia asked, surprised, and then realized she'd destroyed the opportunity her cousin had afforded her to appear the damsel in distress. Though after a moment's reflection she realized she wanted Mr. Hartwell to know the truth, to see if he could still admire her once he became aware of how very flawed she was. So she admitted, "It wasn't *just* my mother's idea. She put no undue pressure on me. I thought at first I would enjoy becoming a viscountess, with all the privileges that entails. But I began to realize that those things matter not at all when weighed against the bigger question of whether or not you can find happiness with a certain person."

"And—do you think you could find happiness with me?" Mr. Hartwell asked nervously, and Cecilia had the traitorous thought that she'd always envisioned her dream man as someone masterful and self-assured. That is, when she wasn't picturing him as a wealthy lord of the realm. But she forced herself to dismiss such thoughts and answered truthfully, "I *think* I can, but I'm not sure." She found that though she had believed herself so very certain she wanted to marry Mr. Hartwell when he no longer wanted to marry *her*, now that he was hers for the asking, her former doubts had quickly returned.

"What do you think it would take to make you sure?" Mr. Hartwell asked, and Cecilia just shook her head, embarrassed to admit that she did not know, that as fond as she was of him, she still felt as if she could be missing out on something better if she committed herself irrevocably, and she was reluctant to do so. However, she was saved from having to explain herself further, because when she shook her head she neglected to look where she was walking and kicked some stone paving, causing her to cry out in pain.

"Oh, ow!" she howled.

"Cecilia! What is it? What is the matter?" Mr. Hartwell asked, wonderfully concerned.

"My toe," Cecilia managed to say between gritted teeth, as she pulled up her skirts slightly and lifted her injured foot to take the weight off of it. Before she could do anything else, she was shocked by Mr. Hartwell lifting her in his arms as if she weighed no more than a child.

"What are you doing?" she asked him, though it was fairly obvious what was happening when she found herself clasped against his chest.

"I am carrying you. So that you do not put any weight on your injured foot." He turned in a complete circle, still holding her, searching the small walled garden for somewhere to sit. He turned so quickly that Cecilia put her hand against his chest in protest saying, "Mr. Hartwell, you are making me dizzy." Then, realizing she was actually touching a man's *chest*, she pulled her hand back as if she'd burnt it.

Mr. Hartwell had not noticed, so intent was he on finding somewhere to set his precious burden. But when it became obvious there was no such place nearby, he lowered himself to the ground with her in his lap. This was much too much for Cecilia, who had almost forgotten her hurt toe, so shocked was she by what had happened next. "Mr. Hartwell!" she protested, finding herself both scandalized and delighted, though unsure which feeling was the predominant one.

Mr. Hartwell suddenly became aware of the impropriety of what he had done, as well as his current position, sitting on the grass in a walled and secluded garden, the woman he loved in his lap. But he still put Cecilia's comfort above everything else. "How is your foot? Are you still in much pain?" he asked her.

Cecilia wasn't even aware she possessed a foot, though she was becoming aware of other portions of her anatomy she hadn't known existed prior to this experience. She just stared at him without replying, his face so close to her own that she could feel his breath tickling her ear, conscious that her chest was pressed against his and that his heart was beating wildly, as if it were about to explode. Or was that her own?

"Cecilia," Mr. Hartwell whispered, and she realized he had now used her Christian name more than once, though he'd never done so before today. And then he took a far greater liberty, pressing his lips against her own.

He drew back far too quickly to please Cecilia, who had forgotten she was supposed to protest such an action. But then, after studying her face in silence for a moment as he held it gently cradled in his hands, he kissed her again.

Cecilia was completely lost to time and place, and later blushed to realize she was not the one to call a halt to such improper behavior but would have eagerly continued until the rest of the party found them. Thankfully, Mr. Hartwell was far too much the gentleman to take advantage of the situation before it progressed any further, and he pulled away, even gently resisting when Cecilia attempted to pull his head back down and raised her lips to his.

"No, Cecilia, we must not, this is not right; I do beg your pardon. But you're so sweet, and I—but I shouldn't say anything more until I've spoken to your mother. I'll do so immediately—" he said, and Cecilia was abruptly returned to her senses when she heard the words "your mother."

"Oh, God, what am I doing? Mr. Hartwell, what must you think of me?" Cecilia asked, horrified, and scrambled out of his lap and onto her feet, heedless of any pain, as her bruised toe now seemed the least of her concerns.

Mr. Hartwell got to his feet as well, brushing himself off. "Cecilia, I will tell you exactly what I think of you as soon as I have your mother's permission. And I will show you as well," he said, his voice deepening.

"But, I told you, I am not sure . . ." Cecilia said, her voice trailing off as she saw Mr. Hartwell's fond expression change to one of disbelief.

"You certainly did not act just now as if you were 'not

sure.' Good God, Cecilia, you can't go on and on encouraging a fellow, and kissing him, and then expect him to run away like a blasted puppy until you whistle for him again. I won't be treated like a dashed Pekingese!" He was glaring at her and Cecilia realized how terribly she'd spoiled the moment.

"You are right. I am so sorry; I don't know what came over me. You've been so patient with me and I've been horrible to you," she said. "It is no wonder you like Emily Woodford."

"*She* appreciates me, at least. If I were to propose to her, she wouldn't hesitate for one second to accept," he replied. And while it wasn't the most mature of comments, Mr. Hartwell was only three-and-twenty himself and had reached the limit of his endurance. "You'd best fix your hair and straighten your bonnet, or you'll be forced to marry me whether you want to or not," he said, and Cecilia was shocked by his discourteous tone. She stood there blinking at him, trying to reconcile this passionate, angry gentleman with the diffident, shy young man who had patiently accepted her offhand and thoughtless treatment of him. But apparently he would accept it no more. Still, as she stood there, fumbling with her hair and her bonnet, his innate kindness came to the fore and he approached her, tenderly tucking back her hair with fingers that trembled. Cecilia trembled, too, at his touch, and was tempted to tell him he could speak to her mother, just so he would kiss her again. But something inside her balked at uttering those fateful words and the moment was soon over. Mr.

Hartwell stepped back, holding out his arm for her to lean upon with a curt reminder not to put too much weight on her foot.

The other couple, secluded in their floral-scented bower, were also coming to a realization of the impropriety of their behavior. Sir Edmund drew back, after one lingering kiss, and met Sophie's wondering gaze. She smiled at him but did not want to be the first to speak. He did not seem disposed to speak, either, and Sophie's smile began to fade as the silence went on a little too long.

"Was that another lesson in flirtation?" Sir Edmund finally asked, with a lightness that seemed forced.

Sophie did not find the remark at all humorous. He still had his arms loosely around her, so she drew away from him completely before replying, "I would never presume to take flirtation so far."

"I beg your pardon," Sir Edmund said. "That was a terrible thing to say, especially as the entire . . . incident occurred at my instigation. Please forgive me. But your nearness, and the romantic setting"—he waved his hand to encompass the beauty around them—"it's no excuse, I know, but I temporarily lost my head. I *sincerely* beg your pardon."

This was not at all what Sophie had expected to hear; she had been poised to accept at the very least a declaration of love and quite possibly a proposal of marriage, and so was conscious of the most crushing disappointment. She could not believe it was all happening again, with an entirely different gentleman, and wondered what was wrong with her that she could apparently inspire admiration but not commitment. She just wanted to get out of the garden and out of Sir Edmund's presence as quickly as possible and jumped up from the bench with that objective in mind.

"Sophie, wait," Sir Edmund said, rising from the bench as well, and Sophie cast him a withering look, wondering how he continued to presume to use her Christian name without permission. Was that the problem? When she had made no issue of that, had he assumed he could take greater liberties with her? But he must have read the significance of her glance, because he quickly corrected himself. "Miss Lattimore, please, there is something I must explain to you. Something similar to what you confided to me about Mr. Maitland."

But Sophie was in no mood to hear any explanations and so murmured, "I'm sorry, I pray you will excuse me." She walked quickly back into the parterre gardens, followed by Sir Edmund, who still attempted to make apologies and explanations until they met Cecilia and Mr. Hartwell making their way back to the house and Sir Edmund realized there would be no further opportunity for private conversation.

If Mrs. Foster found the subsequent behavior of her daughter and niece strange, she knew better than to remark upon it. Cecilia, of course, had the excuse that she had hurt her foot, and she *was* limping slightly, so that might have accounted for her very serious, unhappy expression, but it did not account for the fact that Mr. Hartwell dropped Cecilia's arm as soon as he had led her safely to a chair in the drawing room and announced that he was leaving to ride back to town.

Sophie, too, was behaving in a most peculiar manner, refusing to look in her host's direction even as she thanked him for his hospitality but insisted that they must leave as well.

"Now that Cecilia has hurt her foot, it would be better if we returned home, where I can apply a cool compress to the injury," she said, and when Sir Edmund said he'd be happy to supply whatever Miss Foster needed, Sophie abruptly interrupted him, still without looking at him, and said, "Thank you, but she'd be more comfortable in her own room, would you not, Cecilia?"

Cecilia, who seemed sunk into gloom, had apparently heard none of this conversation, and it had to be repeated to her before she agreed vehemently that she wanted nothing more than to go home.

Sir Edmund expressed his hope that they would at least stay for tea, and Mrs. Foster had a similar hope, but her niece and daughter would not hear of it and rose to take their leave.

"But what about Mrs. Beswick?" Mrs. Foster ventured to protest. "She has not yet returned to the house."

However, even as she said it, Priscilla entered the drawing room on her husband's arm. Though they didn't appear to be enthralled with each other—Charles Beswick was wearing his usual expression of boredom—they did appear to be the only couple to have remained upon speaking terms after their excursion together. Though Mrs. Foster did wonder how long that state of affairs would continue when Priscilla announced, "I hope we do not reek of horses; Charles *insisted* upon looking over every one."

Before she could say anything else, Sophie informed Priscilla that they were leaving immediately, deaf to Priscilla's protests that she thought they were to stay for tea. "Cecilia has hurt herself," Sophie said in brief explanation, before curtsying to Sir Edmund in an obvious farewell. "Thank you, Sir Edmund, for your hospitality and for the tour of your house. Newbrooke is lovely." But as this was said in a polite but wooden tone, Mrs. Foster did not think it sounded very convincing, and so she made her own compliments and thanks in a much more enthusiastic tone of voice, in an attempt to make up for her niece's inexplicable behavior.

Sir Edmund was left facing his very confused housekeeper upon the departure of all of his guests. "But, Sir Edmund, I thought you said tea was to be served in the Yellow Drawing Room at five o'clock."

"I beg your pardon, Mrs. Cooper, it was a miscommunication on my part. Pray forgive me; I know it has caused you great inconvenience. Perhaps the staff would enjoy having tea in the servants' hall," he offered, but he knew it was very small consolation. The servants had all outdone themselves to present Newbrooke in the best possible light, hav-

ing come to be aware, he knew not how, that there was a
special young lady to tour the house that day, a lady who
might, in the near future, become their mistress.

He couldn't face their disappointed and commiserating
looks, so he asked for his horse and rode for over an hour,
little conscious of where he went, but not surprised at the
end of it to find himself in a certain alcove, rubbing a satiny
rose petal with one finger and thinking how similar it was—
but how much it paled in comparison—to her smooth, delicate skin.

He did not know what had possessed him to make
such an insulting remark. He had as good as accused her
of being a coquette, when *he* had been the one to kiss *her*!
It was the kiss that had caused all of his problems. He'd had
no intention of kissing her until they were engaged, and no
intention of becoming engaged until he had explained his
past. It had been an unthinking reaction to her proximity,
to having her so near him, her lips just inches away . . .
Why was he trying to fool himself? He would do it again
if she were here now.

And really, if he hadn't made that offhand remark, the
kiss wouldn't have been so terrible. Terrible? It had been
wonderful. No, he couldn't regret that kiss. It was something precious to remember if he were to have nothing
else.

If only he had not panicked and angered her with his
thoughtless remark. He had not meant what she'd obviously assumed, that he was accusing her of light behavior,
of being the type of woman he meant only to trifle with and

toward whom he had no serious intentions. She must think him worse than her first beau, that dastardly Maitland!

But he *had* panicked; thinking that things were progressing too fast, he had tried to lighten the charged atmosphere before returning to their previous conversation. His intention was to make a full confession of his past before proceeding any further. Rather than doing so, however, he had repeatedly apologized for kissing her, as if it had been something distasteful! It was no wonder she had been so upset! If he hadn't handled things so badly they might be in the drawing room now, opening a bottle of champagne and celebrating their engagement. Instead, he did not know if she would ever speak to him again.

The drive back to Bath was most definitely not spent in carefree and joyous conversation, as the drive to Newbrooke had been, and thus seemed much longer to the four women trapped together in the carriage. Priscilla, who had never learned that there were times when you should not state the obvious, attempted to remark upon Sophie's strange behavior, but was the recipient of the most awesome and ferocious glare she'd ever seen upon Sophie's typically mild and pleasant countenance, so that even she was cowed to silence.

However, Priscilla could never be quiet for long and decided Cecilia might be more inclined to converse. "How did you hurt your foot, Cecilia?" Priscilla asked her.

But this did not appear to be a successful conversational gambit, either, as Cecilia blushed fiery red before saying, "I hit it on a stone, and would prefer not to discuss it."

Even Priscilla found it difficult to persist in the face of this determined set down and, after exchanging a perplexed look with Mrs. Foster, turned to stare out the carriage window, resolved not to speak again until she was dropped off on her doorstep. However, this resolution was broken once they reached the city. They were just about to pass Molland's, the confectionary shop, when a child darted into the road and the coachman had to temporarily stop the horses until order was restored. Priscilla, who could see directly into the shop window, was surprised to see someone she knew and exclaimed to the others, "Look! It is Mr. Maitland and Lady Mary!"

The women all looked out the window at her exclamation, but Sophie was the only one on the same side of the carriage as Priscilla and so found herself facing Mr. Maitland at the very moment when he looked out the shop window directly at her. It wasn't just he and Lady Mary who were in the shop, Sophie noticed; his children and their nurse were also present. Sophie was a little embarrassed to be caught gawking at them, but Mr. Maitland did not seem at all disconcerted at being observed. On the contrary, he appeared happy to see Sophie and smiled brilliantly at her, nodding his head in greeting. Sophie nodded slightly in response before the coachman started the horses again and they disappeared from view.

"Well! I would never have thought Mr. Maitland would

go on the strut with Lady Mary!" Priscilla said, seemingly offended that one of her *soi-disant* admirers would appear in public with a woman with no claim to beauty.

"The children like her," Sophie said, confident that was the reason for the outing, as hadn't Mr. Maitland told her that he did not think Lady Mary at all handsome? Sophie was not jealous of Lady Mary in the least, reflecting that if there was any woman she had reason to fear would steal Mr. Maitland's affections from her it was Priscilla herself, who seemed to have an unusual rapport with him. Not that it mattered anyway, because hadn't Sophie just promised Sir Edmund that she would never marry Mr. Maitland? Oh, Lord, had she really? What on earth was wrong with her? She was going to lose both her beaux and die a lonely old maid.

And the other inhabitants of the carriage were quite startled when Sophie made a faint sound of distress and dropped her head into her hands.

14

$\mathcal{S}$ophie, who had gone up to her room as soon as they returned from Newbrooke and was determined to spend the rest of her life lying in bed, was thwarted in this endeavor by the sound of a knock at her bedchamber door.

She had no doubt that it was Cecilia, come to talk to her about her own relationship troubles, as it was quite apparent to Sophie that something momentous had occurred between her and Mr. Hartwell in the gardens. Sophie wished that she had an older confidant whom she could rely on for solace and support as Cecilia did with her, but then told herself that helping Cecilia would at least take her mind off her own problems, and she had no doubt that whatever had occurred between the young couple could easily be rectified, unlike her own situation, which appeared bleak indeed.

So she willingly opened the door for Cecilia and they both settled in comfortably for a long talk, though Cecilia seemed hesitant to begin. Sophie had to prompt her by asking, "Cecilia, what happened between you and Mr. Hartwell at Newbrooke?"

"He kissed me, and now he's going to marry Emily Woodford!" After this pronouncement Cecilia looked as if she was about to cry, and so Sophie had to wait some time for an explanation of this highly unlikely description of Mr. Hartwell's behavior, which Sophie found she could not quite believe.

Finally, Cecilia composed herself enough to explain how she had hurt her foot, and how Mr. Hartwell had kindly picked her up so that she would not injure herself further. The part where she ended up in his lap with them passionately kissing each other was glossed over, so that Sophie received a highly edited and more proper account than what had actually occurred, but there were enough details for her to realize that Newbrooke's gardens were more potent than one of Cupid's arrows in inciting romantic behavior.

Cecilia then came to the crux of her and Mr. Hartwell's disagreement, which was that she had not allowed Mr. Hartwell to approach her mother to ask permission to propose and he had become angry with her and accused her of leading him on. "And indeed I did, but I had no idea; I mean, I had never been kissed before and had not expected it to be quite so . . . exhilarating," Cecilia said, her brow wrinkled in confusion at her own behavior.

"And that was when he announced that he was going to marry Emily Woodford instead?" Sophie asked, still flummoxed by this part of the story.

"That is not what he said, exactly," Cecilia admitted. "In fact, I think *I* was the one who introduced her into the conversation. But he then said that at least *she* appreciated him and that she would not hesitate for one second to accept him. I think I may have driven him into her arms," Cecilia said sadly, before finishing with the obscure remark, "And he even fixed my hair!"

Sophie did not demand an explanation for this non sequitur, instead focusing on what she felt was the heart of the matter. "Cecilia, are you still unsure whether or not you wish to marry Mr. Hartwell? Because I think if you permitted him to speak to your mother this entire disagreement could be happily resolved. And I thought you *had* decided you loved him and wanted to marry him."

"I had, but that was when I thought he was lost to me. Now that I'm faced with accepting his proposal I find myself terrified at committing myself irrevocably. I *am* very fond of him and I missed him dreadfully when he stopped calling, but I also hate the thought of having all my options taken away. What if I've mistaken my feelings and Mr. Hartwell is *not* the right one? It's such an important decision, Sophie. It's for *forever*."

Sophie couldn't deny the truth of Cecilia's words. It *was* an important decision, one of the most important of a person's life. And even more so for a woman than a man, because a woman had no rights other than those her husband granted her. If he wished, he could make her life miserable indeed.

Not that Cecilia need fear Mr. Hartwell would be an overly demanding husband. His kindness and gentleness shone through everything he said and did. Still, if Cecilia did not feel, at eighteen, that she was ready to take such an irrevocable step, then Sophie felt she probably shouldn't.

Cecilia broke the thoughtful silence the two girls had fallen into. "There is one thing, however, that I have not the *slightest* doubt of: I am *very* sure that I do not want him marrying anyone else."

This statement caused Sophie to suddenly feel far more sympathy for Mr. Hartwell than for her cousin.

Now that Cecilia had recovered from her indisposition, the ladies could not continue to spend their time locked inside their town house, even though they had little desire to socialize. Still, appearances must be kept, and Mrs. Foster had announced they were all to attend the assembly rooms that evening.

Sophie consoled herself with the fact that Sir Edmund was unlikely to be present, as she very much doubted he would have so quickly left his estate to return to Bath. But she found that, instead of providing consolation, such a conclusion depressed her even further.

Cecilia was in a worse state than Sophie; not only was she unsure if she would encounter Mr. Hartwell that evening but she feared that if she did see him, he would be paying court to Emily Woodford. This would also be her first meeting with Lord Courtney since she had decided against marrying him, and she had no idea how to tactfully convey a rejection to a suitor she had so willingly encouraged little more than a week ago.

And Mrs. Foster, who was the one to insist upon their attendance in the first place, was perhaps the most apprehensive of the three women. For she had to somehow back away from her chummy behavior with Lady Smallpeace and her tacit acceptance of Lord Courtney as a husband for her daughter without alienating the noblewoman completely and committing social suicide.

As matters turned out, when they entered the assembly rooms Lady Smallpeace spied them almost immediately, and inquired very loudly and tactlessly about Cecilia's health.

"How is your daughter, Mrs. Foster? Has she recovered from her indisposition? Looks a little pale, if you ask me," Lady Smallpeace said, raising her lorgnette to her eyes and looking Cecilia up and down.

"She is much improved, thank you," Mrs. Foster responded.

"Positively blooming," Lord Courtney said, with a smirk. "Mustn't come too close or I might sneeze," he said, and his aunt dropped her lorgnette.

"Is she still contagious, do you think?" Lady Smallpeace asked, horrified.

"No, Aunt, it was just a small jest, a play on words. Flowers make me sneeze and Miss Foster is *blooming*, like a daisy, though maybe not a daisy, as she's wearing blue. Perhaps a bluebell? Don't know much about flowers, other than the fact my nose itches around them. That reminds me, hope you liked that bouquet I sent you, Miss Foster. Had my man select it for you especially—"

His great-aunt interrupted before Cecilia could thank Lord Courtney for his servant's gift. "Is your daughter *prone* to infections, Mrs. Foster?" Lady Smallpeace asked, an expression of revulsion on her face.

And Mrs. Foster was suddenly overcome by a notion so brilliant, she felt as if light should be radiating from her head. "I am afraid so, Lady Smallpeace," she said. Cecilia jumped in surprise and looked as if she was about to protest, but Sophie, who had figured out her aunt's clever scheme, squeezed Cecilia's arm in warning. "She has been in delicate health since a particularly bad case of a putrid sore throat when she was fourteen. A surgeon was called in and he said it was likely that her constitution was permanently weakened." Mrs. Foster managed to look quite woebegone as she said this, and Sophie and Cecilia composed their features into suitably serious expressions as well.

"Upon my word!" Lady Smallpeace said, looking at Cecilia with a strange mixture of pity, disgust, and relief. "I am very glad I learned of this! *Very* glad! I am sorry, young lady, but I must ask you to keep your distance until we are quite sure you are recovered from this latest infectious illness. I know my nephew will be quite disappointed not to be able to dance with you this evening, won't you, Courtney?"

"Devastated," he said, smiling. "Perhaps tomorrow—"

"Courtney!" Lady Smallpeace shouted. "Your arm!"

And as the ladies watched in amazement, Lady Small-peace heaved herself out of her chair and got up to leave the room. Sophie realized that this was the first time she'd actually seen Lady Smallpeace walk. Lady Mary took her mother's other arm, offering excuses and apologies as they walked away.

"So sorry, but my mother, quite a dread of illness, though her constitution is quite strong. Like a horse. Is that the correct expression? Or is it a mule? I am not much of a horsewoman myself, though I do ride in the country. No need for it here in Bath, of course, much easier to get a chair, and so many hills, a horse *would* need a strong con-stitution if one were to ride here . . ."

The three ladies stood silently for a moment longer af-ter Lady Mary's voice had trailed away, and then Sophie began laughing.

"That was brilliant, Aunt Foster!" Sophie congratu-lated her aunt. "What quick thinking!"

"Mama, how *did* you think of such a thing? Now we needn't avoid them; they will avoid us!"

"It just came to me," Mrs. Foster said happily.

Mr. Hartwell was not present that evening, though Emily Woodford was. Cecilia nodded very graciously and even smiled at Emily when she approached them, but was en-gaged for a set and left soon afterward. After Cecilia was gone, Emily turned eagerly to speak to Sophie.

"Sophie! It's been an age since we've last talked. I heard your cousin was ill."

"Yes, but it was only a cold. She's fine now."

"That's not what I heard. There's a rumor going around that she's . . . *consumptive*," Emily said, her voice dropping down to a whisper on the last word.

"Nonsense! Why, Cecilia is as healthy as a horse," Sophie said, chuckling a little as she thought of Lady Mary's use of that expression. Emily looked at Sophie strangely, as if she felt her cousin's health was no laughing matter, but let the subject drop.

"Well, I'm happy that Miss Foster is better. Perhaps now her suitors will resume calling on her," Emily said, trying to look as if she were casually introducing the subject of Cecilia's suitors into the conversation, and not as if it were the entire reason she'd approached Sophie in the first place. "Have you seen anything of Mr. Hartwell recently?"

Sophie was torn. She did like Emily, and for all she knew she would make Mr. Hartwell a wonderful wife. That is, if Cecilia ever decided she didn't want him for herself. But Sophie felt *that* should be resolved before he became involved with someone else. "Yes, Emily, we have seen Mr. Hartwell recently. As I mentioned before, he and Cecilia—"

"What about them? Did he propose? Are they engaged?" Emily asked urgently.

"They are not engaged *yet*," Sophie said, thinking perhaps this conversation was a mistake after all. The ordinarily docile Emily seemed quite the opposite of her usual calm self.

"If they are not engaged, there's still hope for me," Emily said, and Sophie's heart sank.

"But Emily, if he is in love with Cecilia—"

"Perhaps he is infatuated with your cousin, but she does not deserve him," Emily said.

"And you do?" Sophie asked.

"Why not? You, of all people, should understand. Mr. Hartwell is young and handsome and comfortably well-off and has no need to marry a lady of fortune. Such men do not grow on trees, Sophie, as you very well know. Yet your cousin hadn't the wit to recognize the gift that had fallen into her lap! She deserves Lord Courtney; she obviously cares more for the title than the man. And as I *do* suitably appreciate Mr. Hartwell, I mean to have him."

Sophie found herself bereft of speech. She could merely blink at her erstwhile friend and rue the day she'd introduced her to Mr. Hartwell. For if Cecilia eventually came to her senses and decided she did want him, it could very well be too late.

Priscilla Beswick had also come to the assembly rooms that evening, and Sophie ran into her in the tea room. She greeted Priscilla with a smile, completely forgetting that the last time she'd seen Priscilla she'd treated her less than cordially.

"I am surprised to find you here. You did not seem to

be in the best of moods after our visit to Newbrooke," Priscilla said, frowning.

"Oh, yes, I apologize. I had the headache. I am better now."

"Cecilia seems to have made a remarkable recovery as well," Priscilla mentioned, looking past Sophie to where Cecilia sat chatting with an admirer.

"It was only a cold—" Sophie began, wondering how often she was going to have to discuss her cousin's health.

"I meant her foot. She had injured herself, had she not?"

"Oh, that! Yes, she is much better."

"Well, I am glad you are here, because I must discuss something with you," Priscilla said, looking to see who was seated around them before lowering her voice. "Charles is absolutely impossible! I tell you, Sophie, I am tempted to do something desperate!"

Sophie sighed, wishing she could have at least a few minutes to enjoy her tea without having to discuss men or marriage. "Priscilla, I do believe Charles has reason to complain about *you* as well. He told me he misses the time you used to spend together in outdoor pursuits. And now, when he does spend time with you, you're always fretting about doing anything that might muss your clothes. Why is it that you no longer participate in any of those activities that you used to enjoy together?"

Priscilla blinked in surprise. "I told you, it's because I discovered that it's inappropriate behavior for a young lady of quality. And indeed, when I went to London for my season and became more involved in ladylike pursuits, the

gentlemen admired me more than ever. And I enjoy fashion, Sophie. I had no idea, until I made my debut, what fun
it was. There is an . . . *art* to it, you know. I have even tried
my hand at my own designs. In fact, the hat I wore to Sydney Gardens was one I had designed myself. That's why I
was particularly upset when it was destroyed." Priscilla
suddenly seemed unsure and hesitant; an attitude Sophie
had never before seen her display. "Perhaps," she suggested
tentatively, "you might like to see some of my sketches."

"I would very much like to see your sketches! It's obvious you have a talent for design; one can tell that by looking at you." Priscilla beamed at this remark and Sophie
began to wonder if Priscilla sought compliments on her
appearance not because of personal vanity, but because
she wanted reassurance about the designs she created.
"But don't you miss those activities you and Charles used
to do together? It sounded as if you enjoyed them."

Priscilla thought for a moment and then a reminiscent
smile appeared. "Yes, I did enjoy riding, and cricket, and
bowls—oh, we used to have such fun! I even enjoyed when
Charles would show me the animals on the farm. But that
was before I was *out*. Surely behavior like that, which is acceptable for a very young woman, is not acceptable for a
married lady."

"Certainly it is, if that's what she and her husband enjoy
doing together! Priscilla, you can be ladylike and fashionable and still engage in sports. I promise you, if you were
to enter more into your husband's interests, he would respond positively."

"That might be true, and when we return to the country I will be sure to do so, but if Charles loves me, why can't he be supportive of *my* interests as well? He has not been to one ball with me since we were married. He even refused to accompany me tonight; Mr. Maitland escorted me here. Surely, if he expects me to ride with him, he could dance with me occasionally!"

Sophie could not deny this was true and vowed to herself to counsel Charles Beswick on this matter at the next opportunity. For now, she encouraged Priscilla to be patient. "Mr. Beswick is a very attractive, intelligent gentleman, Priscilla, and he loves you very much. Indeed, he told me so himself."

"He did?" Priscilla asked, clapping her hands together in delight. "What exactly did he say?" she demanded.

"That he loved you very much," Sophie repeated, thinking that she was very ill-equipped for this role she'd reluctantly assumed. She should have read poetry or romance novels to prepare herself.

"Was he wearing his blue coat?" Priscilla asked, a dreamy expression on her face.

"Yes," Sophie said, and took a sip of tea.

Sophie had not been aware that Mr. Maitland was Priscilla's escort that evening until Priscilla told her so. She really hoped when Priscilla mentioned doing something "desperate" it did not involve him. But Sophie strongly believed that Priscilla really did love her husband, and though she might be a little immature, she wasn't immoral. If she felt it was socially unacceptable for a lady to dirty her hem visiting the stables, certainly she knew it was far worse to leave your husband and elope with another man.

Mr. Maitland was strangely reticent with Sophie that evening, giving Priscilla Beswick most of his attention while casting significant glances in Sophie's direction. She could only assume he was trying to make her jealous, though perhaps she was flattering herself. But she could not muster the energy to feel any outrage, as she had apparently expended it all on Sir Edmund earlier that day. She'd had quite enough of men for the present, and as Cecilia felt the same, the ladies decided to leave after tea. They all felt they'd accomplished their purpose that evening, which was to show their faces and discourage Lord Courtney's suit without becoming social outcasts in the process.

It was only after they returned home that Mrs. Foster told Sophie Mr. Maitland had spoken to her and asked permission to pay his addresses to Sophie the following day.

"Pay his addresses!" Cecilia repeated, shocked. "Sophie, he means to propose!"

Sophie was no less shocked, even though she realized she should not be. Certainly Mr. Maitland had courted her so assiduously that if he had drawn back again he would not have been able to retain his standing as a gentleman.

But instead of feeling that this was the culmination of her life's dreams, a vindication for eighteen-year-old Sophie, who had been publicly humiliated and made to feel unwanted, unattractive, and unimportant, she instead felt . . . nothing.

"What answer will you give him?" Cecilia asked.

"I don't know," Sophie replied.

15

Sophie's strange ambivalence lasted through the night and into the next day. She had breakfasted, dressed, and was awaiting Mr. Maitland's call in the drawing room and still had no idea what reply to make to his offer. She discounted the promise she'd made to Sir Edmund that she wouldn't marry Mr. Maitland; he had no right to demand promises *of* her when he apparently felt no obligation to make them *to* her. Really, it should be easier now that Sir Edmund had taken himself out of the running for her hand. She only had two options: marriage to Mr. Maitland, whom she had loved once and still found charming and extremely attractive, or lonely spinsterhood.

Maybe I should reread "Advice to Sophronia" for guidance, Sophie thought to herself, and this at least made her smile.

Cecilia and Mrs. Foster had not pleaded for or against Mr. Maitland. After Sophie told Cecilia that she did not know what answer she would give him, Mrs. Foster had said: "You've proven yourself to be a good judge of character, Sophie, much better than either Cecilia or I. So I have no doubt that whatever decision you make will be the right one."

Sophie was left feeling gratified by the unusual praise from her aunt, while wishing at the same time she had told Sophie exactly what she should do.

Now Sophie was restlessly pacing back and forth, finally going over to stand in front of the portrait of the lady in the ruff, tempted to ask *her* for advice. Before she could do so, Mr. Maitland was finally announced.

She turned to greet him, and was struck again by how very good-looking he was. He was wearing a gray coat, a color he had to know emphasized the incredible blue of his eyes, and *two* waistcoats, a pink one and a patterned silk, and Sophie realized that he had probably taken even more pains with his appearance than she had. It was unbelievable to her that such a handsome man considered *her* a desirable wife, but as she had no fortune and he was no longer in need of one, he could only be choosing her because he wanted to. She started comparing him mentally to Sir Edmund, telling herself Mr. Maitland was the more handsome—and he was—before realizing it did not matter anyway; she was no longer deciding between the two men and must stop thinking of Sir Edmund and instead think only of the man standing before her. And certainly, if a woman had Frederick Maitland, she was in need of no other man.

So she offered him her hand with a smile as composed as she could make it, especially when he raised her hand to his lips, a liberty he had seldom taken before now.

"Sophie," he said, still holding her hand in his and reaching out to grasp the other. "I've dreamt so long of this day, that I can scarcely believe this is really happening."

Sophie felt the first stirring of emotion pierce the numbness that had overtaken her, but it was not the emotion she had expected to feel. Instead of wonder, happiness, affection, or even passion, she felt . . . anger.

How dare he! *He'd* dreamt for so long! she thought, wrenching her hands from his.

"And when did you dream of it? Before or after your marriage to another woman?" she heard herself asking, and it was as if her soul had left her body and taken a seat in the corner of the room and she was watching herself say these bitter things but unable to do anything to stop them from coming out of her mouth.

Maitland winced. "Sophie, what can I say so that you will forgive me? I was wrong, I admit it. My marriage was not a happy one. Is that what you want to hear? But she was so persistent in her admiration for me, and you were so young; I was never completely sure of your feelings—"

"I don't believe you. Say, rather, the truth: she had money and I had none."

"That was part of it, undoubtedly," Maitland agreed,

his tone calm and affectionate, which somehow made Sophie feel as if *she* was being cast as the unreasonable party in this affair. "Who of us does not, cannot, consider such things? Tell me, Sophie, if I came to you now and had nothing, would you even entertain my suit? Of course not! You would not be able to, even if you wished to."

"If I'd had money of my own, as you did, and we truly loved each other, I would have been happy to share what I had with you."

Maitland smiled tenderly at her. "This is why I love you, Sophie. You're so pure at heart, so untainted by the worldly considerations that influence the rest of us."

Sophie thought this was a somewhat unromantic reason; it made her feel rather like a pious nun. She wasn't so unworldly that she wouldn't rather hear praise of her eyes or lips. Sir Edmund had told her that she was lovely, at least. Maitland must have sensed her disappointment; he was so attuned to his audience, always reading them and adjusting himself to fit their response. He raised his hand to her mouth and traced her lips with one finger, and Sophie was disconcerted to feel something other than anger, something more akin to passion.

"But I'm not pure at heart like you, Sophie. It's not just your inner qualities that I find so appealing," he said huskily, before bending and kissing her.

Sophie found it quite astonishing that she had gone eight-and-twenty years without being kissed by even one gentleman and had now been kissed by two different ones in the span of as many days. It was odd, too, that she'd thoroughly enjoyed both kisses, though when Mr. Maitland kissed her she had a pang of heart, a feeling that she was betraying Sir Edmund, which was absolutely absurd, as he was nothing to her. So she dismissed that feeling and concentrated on the other feelings Mr. Maitland was stirring inside of her, which were tumultuous indeed.

He drew back after a moment, smiling triumphantly. "I shall put a notice in the papers immediately," he said, and Sophie realized he'd assumed her acceptance of his embrace meant she'd also accepted his proposal. "And, Sophie, love, don't you think you could finally call me Frederick?"

"Wait! Mr. Maitland—Frederick," she amended, as it did seem hypocritical to continue mistering a man who had just kissed her, "I have not yet accepted your proposal."

"Oh, Lord, I didn't actually ask the question, did I? I do beg your pardon, Sophie, but it's your fault, you know, for being so distracting. Should I go down on one knee?" he asked, and began looking down at the floor as if preparing to do so.

"No, that's not why—that is, I am aware of your purpose in calling this morning, it is just that I"—and once again she had that out-of-body feeling, the sensation that someone else was saying the words that were inexplicably coming from her mouth—"I *cannot* accept your proposal."

She was as shocked to hear herself say those words as Frederick Maitland was. "You cannot accept my proposal," he repeated.

"At least, not right away. I think I need time," she said, feeling the complete idiot, as they both were aware she'd had more than enough time; and that if he'd asked this question ten years ago there would have been no doubt what her answer would have been.

But he was too perceptive not to realize what was really at issue. "It's Sir Edmund, is it not? You fancy him; I've seen it on your face. But Sophie, if you believe I toyed with your affections and are holding it against me, you must be aware that he did far worse. Surely he told you?"

Sophie wanted to put her hands over her ears, so sure was she that she did not want to hear what he was about to tell her. However, she was eight-and-twenty, not eight. "Told me what?" she asked.

"It's not a pretty tale, and normally I would not sully your ears with it. Certainly it never became widely known in society, even though the gentlemen who were at Cambridge together were aware of it."

"You were at Cambridge?" Sophie asked, as this was the first she'd heard of it, and she was certain he would have managed to mention it before now.

"No, not I. But I was at Eton with a fellow who later went on to Cambridge, and he knew Sir Edmund. It was from him I had the story, and he would not have lied about such a matter."

Sophie was skeptical, but she couldn't help remembering that just yesterday Sir Edmund had said he had something he wanted to explain to her, something "similar to what she'd confided in him." So she refrained from comment, and Maitland continued his explanation.

"There was a young lady who was accepted in Cambridge society though she came from an undistinguished, middle-class family. Still, she was lively and pretty and popular. Sir Edmund began paying her obvious attentions, dancing with her at local assemblies and taking her for drives. But apparently he had no intention of marrying her, something that became very obvious when it became necessary for her to marry and he would not do the proper thing."

"Necessary for her to marry? You mean . . ." Sophie was unsure how to finish the sentence.

"She became pregnant with Sir Edmund's child," Mr. Maitland said bluntly.

"You cannot know that for certain," Sophie protested.

"It is what she asserted, and she would hardly have said such a thing, destroying her own reputation, if it were not true," Mr. Maitland said reasonably. "And his behavior also established his guilt. He paid his steward at New-brooke to marry her. The young woman reportedly gave birth to a healthy baby boy just a few months after their marriage."

"Poor girl," Sophie said.

"It is you I feel sorry for, Sophie, not this girl I've never met. You, the woman I love, who has allowed herself to be manipulated by Sir Edmund."

"I have not been manipulated by him," Sophie protested, but it was said to defend herself, not Sir Edmund.

"Haven't you? Wouldn't you be accepting my proposal right now, if it were not for him?"

Sophie didn't respond; she didn't feel capable of a response. It was all too much to process, and she wished Mr. Maitland would just go away so she could do so.

With his unique gift for perception, Mr. Maitland easily discerned Sophie's feelings. "But I will not persist when you're obviously not in a mood to hear my addresses," he said. "I will give you time, Sophie, since that is what you have asked for, and when I return I trust that I will have the answer I most desire. Because I do love you, my dear, despite my very foolish behavior ten years ago."

And Sophie, though she was in a state of confusion and preoccupied with what she'd just learned about Sir Edmund, could not hear such words without being stirred. However, when he bent to kiss her again she quickly stepped back, offering him her hand instead.

"I'll wait, Sophie, but please don't make me wait *too* long. I think you and I have waited long enough," he said, before pressing a fervent kiss on the hand she'd offered him. And then he was gone.

Cecilia came into the room almost as soon as the door had closed behind Maitland.

"Well?" she asked Sophie. "Am I to congratulate you?"

"For being an idiot? I'm not sure congratulations are in order," Sophie said.

"I don't understand. Are you an idiot for accepting him or for refusing him?"

"For doing neither," Sophie said, shaking her head at her own stupidity. "I asked for more time."

Cecilia dropped onto the sofa beside Sophie. "You are almost as bad as I am," Cecilia told her cousin.

"Don't remind me. Now I can no longer look down upon you with disdain," Sophie said, half joking.

"Is that what you used to do?" Cecilia asked.

Sophie nodded. "We might be cousins, but I am firmly on Mr. Hartwell's side in this matter."

Cecilia sighed. "So am I."

Mrs. Foster had joined the two girls in the drawing room when they heard a second visitor arrive and their manservant came to ask if they were at home to Mr. Hartwell.

Mrs. Foster looked quickly at Cecilia, who nodded.

"Yes, Jonas, you can admit Mr. Hartwell," Mrs. Foster told him, as her daughter rushed to check her appearance in a mirror hanging on the wall.

Cecilia had just rejoined Sophie on the sofa when Mr. Hartwell entered, looking unusually grave.

"Mr. Hartwell, how good of you to call. Please take a seat," Mrs. Foster told him with a smile.

"Thank you, Mrs. Foster, but I wondered if I could beg the indulgence of a word in private with Miss Foster. It should not take long," he said.

This was very irregular behavior, but the events of the past weeks had shaken Mrs. Foster, and she was determined to do nothing to further jeopardize the happiness of her daughter, or even her niece. So she and Sophie quietly got up and left the room.

"I am come to take my leave of you," Mr. Hartwell announced, to Cecilia's great surprise, as she had half expected him to again ask her permission to approach her mother and formalize their relationship, and had wondered, with a delicious thrill, what form his persuasions would take. But a less amorous-looking gentleman she had never seen, as he stood, stern and unsmiling, before her.

"Take your leave?" Cecilia repeated. "Where are you going?"

"To my estate in Derbyshire," he said, to her even greater surprise, as she'd expected him to announce his return to London, where she at least had hopes of seeing him again once they, too, returned there from Bath.

"Your estate in Derbyshire," she said faintly, before realizing she was doing no more than parroting his words and must sound the greatest simpleton alive. "Will you be returning to London after you've completed your business there?"

"No, I am removing there indefinitely. I have no plans to return to London. Or Bath," he added.

"Then, I am *never* to see you again?" Cecilia whispered.

"Perhaps someday," he said. "When it no longer matters."

There was a moment of silence, and then he bowed to her before turning to leave the room.

"Wait!" Cecilia called. He turned back. "Will you write to me?" she asked.

"I do not think that would be appropriate, as we are not related or affianced."

Cecilia walked over to where he stood by the door. "You may kiss me goodbye, if you'd like," she said, tilting her face up toward his and closing her eyes. After a moment, when nothing happened, she opened them. He was staring at her, but it did not seem as if his eyes held the adoration that she was so accustomed to seeing.

"Goodbye, Cecilia," he said, and left the room.

After leaving Cecilia with Mr. Hartwell, Sophie and Mrs. Foster went to the dining room, where they sat together in silence. Sophie wished she'd at least thought to bring her sewing along with her; she had left it on the sofa next to Cecilia. Before she could excuse herself to go to her room and find something else to occupy her, Mrs. Foster turned to Sophie and said, "I'm very pleased to have this opportunity to speak with you alone, Sophie. There is something I've been wanting to say to you."

Mrs. Foster was very obviously ill at ease, and Sophie assumed this was bad news indeed and steeled herself for her aunt's confession.

"I wanted to apologize for the way I treated you after you came to London," Mrs. Foster said. "Cecilia related to me what you told her of your history with Mr. Maitland, of your ostracism from society after his marriage to another, and how you'd failed to find a real home after coming to live with us. I most humbly and sincerely beg your pardon, Sophie. I realize now how you must have felt, completely alone in the world and being treated as an unwelcome encumbrance by the only family you had left. I hope you can forgive me."

"Of course I can forgive you, Aunt. I imagine I *was* an unwelcome encumbrance," Sophie said, with a slight smile. "Another young lady to feed and shelter, with no prospect of ever being rid of her."

"No, Sophie! You mustn't think that! That is the other thing I wished to say. I wanted to assure you that you are a *most* welcome part of this family. Whatever Cecilia decides, whether she marries or not, *I* have decided that I've enjoyed this time in Bath, and indeed there are other places that I quite long to visit. I would hate to do so alone. Even if we were not to travel together but merely return to London, I've come to value your companionship and would miss you exceedingly if you were to leave us. What I'm attempting to say, Sophie, is that I pray you do not marry Mr. Maitland merely to acquire a home, because you have one with me for as long as you may want it. Indeed, if I had my way in the matter, I'd counsel you to reject Mr. Maitland immediately so we could depart on a tour of the Lake District," Mrs. Foster said, and Sophie was astounded that it was said in a droll, humorous tone, as if she were attempting a jest. Aunt Foster, joking! Sophie had never thought she'd see the day.

So Sophie wasn't sure why she was more inclined toward tears than laughter. She surreptitiously wiped at her eyes, and her aunt cleared her throat and looked away, seemingly overcome as well. Sophie's impulse was to hug her aunt, but looking at her as she sat ramrod straight, her face turned away in embarrassment, Sophie realized that it was a little early for affectionate gestures. Maybe after another six years.

Before any more could be said between them, Cecilia ran into the room.

"He is leaving! I am never to see him again," she announced, and burst into tears.

16

*S*ophie felt it impossible that any matchmaker had ever had a more ignominious fall than she had. Not only had she failed to make a match for her own cousin, but she herself, who had recently been courted by two highly eligible gentlemen, was destined to remain a spinster.

For she had decided to reject Frederick Maitland's offer.

She had been sorely tempted to give him an answer in the affirmative, entirely so she could experience what theologians would most likely term "the desires of the flesh." There was no denying his kiss had aroused a passionate response in her, and hadn't Saint Paul said: "it is better to marry than to burn"? But she hadn't been named Sophronia for nothing, and she had the wisdom to realize that marriage with a man whom she did not, *could* not trust; a man who had already caused her a great deal of heartache and had a disconcerting tendency to flirt with other women; was not destined to provide her with any lasting happiness.

The interview was thankfully very brief. It took place the day following Mr. Maitland's proposal, after Sophie had sent him a note requesting that he call. Her aunt Foster was present the entire time, even when Mr. Maitland asked if he and Sophie could be alone together.

"I do not think that is necessary, Mr. Maitland," Sophie replied. "You did me the great honor of making me an offer of marriage that unfortunately I cannot accept. I apologize for any disappointment my refusal may cause you."

"You still haven't given up on trying to catch the richer marital prize, have you, Sophie? Just don't expect me to renew my offer when Sir Edmund fails to come up to scratch," Mr. Maitland said, and Sophie was conscious of a huge feeling of relief that he had reacted in this manner, which had the effect of making her surer than ever that her decision was the right one.

"Mr. Maitland! That is not a very gentlemanly remark," Mrs. Foster protested.

"It is no matter, Aunt," Sophie said. "It is not to be wondered that Mr. Maitland thinks I would be most concerned with marrying for money, when it is what he did himself."

But Mr. Maitland was not one to waste his energy on a hopeless endeavor, and he recognized that Sophie was not going to change her mind. Regaining his usual composure, he made her a very elegant bow. "Goodbye, Sophie, my love. You are making a terrible mistake, you know. But I made a much bigger one, ten years ago, so I suppose

I have only myself to blame." He flashed his charming smile at her, and Sophie felt a sharp twinge of regret at what she was rejecting but managed a cool nod in response, and he soon left the room.

Mrs. Foster looked over at her, a little stunned by what she'd just witnessed. "I must say, Sophie, that I'm not sure I would have had the fortitude to do what you just did. Mr. Maitland is *such* an attractive gentleman! But sadly unreliable. There is no doubt you made the prudent choice," her aunt commended her.

Sophie sighed. "Sometimes I wish my mother had named me 'Clara.' Or 'Jane.'"

"What?" her aunt asked, unable to follow this conversational diversion.

"It's nothing, Aunt," said Sophie, turning to her with a determined smile. "I think you had a brilliant idea earlier. Let's plan a tour of the Lake District."

Before they could plan a trip anywhere, even to Sydney Gardens (as Sophie and Mrs. Foster were determined to get Cecilia out of the house for some fresh air), they had another visitor. But instead of proceeding directly into the drawing room, he could be heard conversing with Jonas in the vestibule.

"That sounds like Sir Edmund," Sophie whispered to her aunt and, though she knew it was foolish, found herself desperately hoping that her suspicion was correct and that it wasn't just the fishmonger or some such person.

"Will you see him?" Mrs. Foster asked, but before Sophie could respond it proved to be a moot point anyway, as Jonas appeared at the door to the drawing room holding a letter.

"Miss Lattimore, Sir Edmund asked if I would pass on this correspondence to you," Jonas said, most formally and properly, though he was undoubtedly aware that it was *not* proper to correspond with a man to whom one was not related or engaged, and that another one of Miss Lattimore's suitors had just left the drawing room only a short while earlier. Sophie was conscious that she was supplying quite a bit of talk for the servants, and that they probably wondered what had happened to the quiet mouse they had grown accustomed to in London.

But Sophie merely replied, "Thank you, Jonas," and held out her hand for the letter. He handed it to her somewhat reluctantly, darting a glance at Mrs. Foster as he did so, his eyebrows raised, as if questioning whether *she* was about to put a stop to such scandalous goings-on.

"That will be all, Jonas," Mrs. Foster barked at him, and Sophie, though she winced at her aunt's tone, could not help feeling grateful for her intervention when Jonas quickly left the room.

"Such insolence!" her aunt remarked. And then, as Sophie still sat with the letter in her hand, making no move to open it, she asked, "Would you like me to leave you to read your letter in solitude?"

Sophie, who had wondered if her aunt would even allow her to read the letter or would take it from her, felt a sudden rush of gratitude and affection for her. It was entirely due to Mrs. Foster that Sophie had the luxury of deciding *if* she would marry and hadn't been forced to accept Mr. Maitland in the face of her many misgivings. And now she was being given similar freedom to decide what action to take toward Sir Edmund.

"Thank you, Aunt, but I'll take it up to my own chamber," she said, and was suddenly consumed with curiosity as to what its contents might be. So after her aunt nodded in dismissal, Sophie fairly flew up the stairs, and was soon reading Sir Edmund's words to her.

The letter had yesterday's date and was written at Newbrooke and began without any salutation:

Now you have not only that impertinence I pressed upon you in the garden but my impertinence in writing this letter to forgive, but I knew no other way to correct the misapprehension I created with my unthinking words, and hoped if I could explain the reason behind my lack of ease with you, and indeed, with all the members of your sex, you could find it in your heart to feel sympathy for me rather than condemnation.

When I was at university I was not the man I am today. I was carefree and perhaps a little careless, I had no fears about raising unfounded expectations in a young woman's mind, and I thought nothing of dancing with and paying court to any lady who took my fancy. Of course, it was all very innocent, or so I thought, until I danced a few too many times or paid a few too many compliments to a young woman who felt she could use my carelessness to her advantage.

She spread the rumor that I had led her to expect an offer of marriage, and her father showed up at my lodgings demanding that I marry his daughter or he would sue me for breach of promise. When I protested that I had never promised her any such thing, he informed me that she was in a delicate condition and that she had claimed the child was mine. I was astounded and told him I was entirely innocent of such charges, that such a thing was impossible, that I had never touched her except to dance with her. I think my honest shock and bewilderment made it obvious to him, at least, that what she said was not true.

When he approached her and told her he knew she had lied, she finally confessed to him that the man who had seduced her had left Cambridge when she'd told him of her condition. By this time, everyone was pressuring me to "do the proper thing" and marry the girl. What was I to do? I couldn't very well go around telling them the truth and thereby destroy her reputation even further. Besides, she would not tell her father who it was who had seduced and abandoned her, probably reasoning that either her father or I would force him to meet us. When she continued to refuse to tell her father who her lover was, he threw her out of the house, a pregnant young woman with nowhere to go. It was unconscionable of him. I heard of it and found her and promised to help. The only solution to her problem that she was interested in was marriage, and I wasn't willing to pay that price. Perhaps you feel I should have done so, but please remember that I was only nineteen! I did not love this girl, and while I had perhaps been a trifle reckless in my behavior, I was not the one responsible for her predicament.

Our steward at Newbrooke at that time was a very ambitious young man, determined to make his fortune, and he had been a natural child himself. I asked him if he'd be willing to marry the young lady if I were to give her a generous dowry. He agreed to it so long as they were able to meet beforehand, to see if they'd suit. They seemed to take to each other immediately and were married as soon as the banns were read. But I had little idea, when I performed such a disinterested act, that this would confirm in people's minds that I was indeed the man who had seduced and abandoned her. I was fortunate that the girl wasn't genteel enough for it to become widely discussed in polite circles, and so I wasn't thrown out of society outright, but it made me extremely hesitant to court any young lady.

Such has been my situation for the past eleven years. I had been forcibly brought to realize that, regardless of any personal attractions, my estate and my wealth made me a desirable catch, and that it behooved me to protect myself from a similar thing happening a second time. But I did desire to marry, most especially when I met you.

Now that you know the reasons for my fears, perhaps you will understand that, while I admired you very much and hoped to court you, I knew not how to do so. I noticed you before we were even introduced, and of course I thought you were lovely—what man would not?—but every time I saw you, even after I'd known you for weeks, I felt this catch in my chest, as if you were literally reaching inside me and touching my heart.

However, I counseled myself to be cautious, and reasoned that if I pretended an interest in having you find me a match, we could continue to meet and I could get to know you better without raising any expectations on your part. Though I think it probably became plain to you very quickly, when I had eyes for no other woman, that it was a ploy and nothing more.

I had thought when I invited you to Newbrooke that if everything went well, I would ask your aunt to allow me to pay my addresses to you. However, you are aware of what happened instead. I pray that you will believe I was not toying with your affections or accusing you of playing the coquette, but I was panicked at the situation proceeding faster than I could control (and at my failure to control myself) and did not know how to react.

I desire nothing more than to prove to you that my intentions toward you are honorable and that nothing in the world would give me greater joy than winning you as my wife. I am no more skilled at explaining my feelings on paper than I am in person, but I have hopefully written enough for you to believe me . . .

Yours ever,
Edmund

Sophie read through the entire letter so quickly that she was convinced she had not read it correctly, and so immediately began reading it a second time as soon as she'd finished it. But she grew impatient reading about Sir Edmund's youthful affair and skipped again to the part where he described his feelings for her, hardly able to believe that he felt that way and had written it down in black and white where it could never be denied.

She sat in her room for some time, marveling over the fact that a scant few hours ago she had turned down Mr. Maitland's offer and had wondered if she was making a dreadful mistake. How quickly everything had changed, now that she knew the man she truly loved returned her affections. Finally, however, she thought about how curious her aunt Foster must be and went downstairs, finding both her and Cecilia eating dinner in the dining room.

Cecilia was pale but composed, even smiling a little when Sophie entered the room. "It is good you came down, as we would have finished it all without you," she said. Then she looked more closely at her cousin. "Sophie, what is it? What happened?"

"Sir Edmund—he wrote—he does have a regard for me—he wants to marry me," Sophie said disjointedly, and her aunt and cousin got up from the table and soon the three ladies were hugging one another, laughing and crying, to the great consternation of the servants, who heard the uproar but were not sure if it portended something good or bad, particularly since both young ladies had been looking utterly miserable the past few days. But when Mrs. Foster called Jonas in to ask that he open a bottle of champagne it was deduced it was definitely good news, and most likely an engagement. However, the servants were not sure if it was Cecilia's or Sophie's betrothal that was being celebrated and which of the four gentlemen who had been courting their young ladies was the lucky man. Finally Jonas, by virtue of his knowledge of "the letter," suggested that it was most likely Sir Edmund who had proposed, and when Betsy put her ear to the dining room door she heard his name mentioned enough that she supported Jonas' theory. And based on the probability of one of their young ladies' marriage to a wealthy baronet the servants opened their own bottle of wine in the kitchen, and were soon making far more noise than that which was emanating from the dining room.

Mrs. Foster was quite perturbed when she did not receive her chocolate the next morning, and Cecilia and Sophie, too, though not as annoyed as she, did wonder where the servants might be and if it was necessary to go down to the kitchen themselves to get a cup of tea. They had finally breakfasted and Sophie, who expected Sir Edmund would call that morning to find out what her reaction had been to his letter, had just put on her best morning gown and had her hair done by a very pale Betsy when she did hear a caller arrive. But upon entering the drawing room she was surprised to find Charles Beswick waiting, and not Sir Edmund.

He had come earlier than was polite, and Sophie's aunt and cousin weren't dressed yet, but Charles had apparently come to see Sophie anyway, and rushed into speech before she could even ask him to sit down.

"I am sorry to call so early, Miss Lattimore, but I was hoping Priscilla might be with you, though I can see that I'm mistaken," he finished, looking around him in despair. "But perhaps you know where she might be?"

"I am sorry, Mr. Beswick, but I have not seen Priscilla since the evening before last, at the assembly rooms," Sophie replied. "She is not at home?"

"She left early this morning," Charles replied. "We quarreled again last night and she is hardly ever up before noon. I can't help thinking she . . . has run off," he said, his voice breaking a little in his distress.

Sophie suddenly remembered that the last time she had seen Priscilla she had mentioned that she might do something "desperate," and so could not immediately assure Charles that his supposition was incorrect. Also, Sophie realized that her rejection of Mr. Maitland's proposal might mean that he, too, felt inclined toward desperate action.

"Oh, no!" Sophie said. "She left no note, no clue as to where she was going?"

Before Charles could answer, there was the sound of another person arriving, and Sophie and Charles looked hopefully toward the door of the drawing room.

"Sir Edmund Winslow," Jonas announced, though his voice was very soft and weak and had tapered off by the end so that it was barely audible. But Sophie had no time to worry about the servants' strange behavior that morning.

Sir Edmund entered the room quickly, a worried expression on his face that turned to one of relief when he saw Sophie. "Thank God!" he said. "I thought you had run off with Maitland."

"What?" Sophie asked, distracted from her shyness at seeing him again by his assumption that she and Maitland had run off together. Why would he think that, unless—

"Did you see Maitland this morning, Sir Edmund?" Charles Beswick asked urgently.

Sir Edmund looked around, as he had not even noticed Charles Beswick, who had walked over to the window when Sir Edmund was announced.

"Yes, which is why I was concerned. I drove here this morning from Newbrooke and passed a coaching inn where I saw Maitland helping a woman into a carriage. She was veiled, so I couldn't see who it was, and she didn't look like Soph—er, Miss Lattimore, but I couldn't think whom Maitland would be escorting out of town and very foolishly began to worry it *was* Miss Lattimore."

He looked again at Sophie. "I beg your pardon for calling so early—"

Charles Beswick interrupted his apologies to announce very matter-of-factly, "It must be Priscilla. She has run off with Maitland."

Sophie had come to the same conclusion herself, little though she wanted to believe it of Priscilla. "We must go after her," she said.

Sir Edmund appeared astounded that he had observed an elopement after all, but Charles, who had suspected it from the start, had gotten over his shock and was now bitterly angry. "She has made her choice very clear," he said. "I will not humiliate myself further by chasing after her."

"But, Mr. Beswick, I am sure she does not love Frederick Maitland, she loves you! She is just young and very foolish. And if she succeeds in running away with him she will be totally ruined! If you love her—"

"If I love her then I am even more foolish than she is, because she's given me no reason to! Please excuse me, Miss Lattimore, Sir Edmund. I have had my fill of Bath. I will be returning to Devon," Charles said, leaving the room before Sophie could stop him.

Edmund and Sophie were left facing each other. "Sir Edmund, you said you drove to town . . ."

"Yes, I have my curricle. Do you want me to go after them?"

"No!" Sophie said, picturing Edmund fighting a duel with Frederick Maitland over Priscilla Beswick. "Not you. I want *us* to go after them. As soon as I change into a carriage dress. That way Priscilla can return with us. That is, if you think we can catch them?"

"Of course we can. He cannot make good time in that ponderous traveling carriage with the team of sorry-looking nags I saw pulling it. I am sure he is headed to London. We'll overtake them in no more than an hour or two."

Sophie, who was already sure she was in love with Sir Edmund, felt it well up inside her to such an extent at this evidence of his goodness that she couldn't stop herself from running over to him and standing on tiptoe to kiss his cheek. "Thank you," she said. Before she could step back he caught her more firmly to him, pressing a longer and more passionate kiss upon her lips.

He drew away slightly to look at her, an expression of adoration on his face, and Sophie thought she might actually burst from happiness. "Sophie, I would chase down a dozen eloping lovers for you."

"It is my sincerest hope that you will not need to, as I am most definitely retiring from my matchmaking career."

"As long as you make *me* a match, with yourself, before you do so," Edmund said. "I assume you read my letter?"

"Yes, and I'm very sorry for what you suffered. We were both greatly affected by the way we were treated in our youth."

"And . . . you will marry me?" he asked, with a resumption of his previous shyness.

"I will," Sophie said, feeling shy herself. But then Edmund lifted her off her feet and swung her around and she began laughing in surprise. As he lowered her to her feet again, he held her so tightly against his chest that she did not feel as if she could breathe, but perhaps that was because she was so very light-headed already. She could feel his heart beating as rapidly as hers and his breathing sounded just as shallow, but she had no desire for him to loosen his hold; she felt as if they could never be close enough. Finally, however, Sophie very reluctantly made herself break away, conscious that every second took Priscilla further away from them. "We should go," she said.

"Yes, we can talk along the way," Sir Edmund said. "You go change. I will wait for you outside."

Sophie explained to her aunt that she was going for a drive with Sir Edmund and that they might also stop at Molland's, so not to expect her back for a few hours. Mrs. Foster, who was in the midst of a domestic crisis, as a strange sickness with symptoms of bloodshot eyes, queasy stomach, and headache had apparently struck all in her employ, merely waved her off with a wish that she enjoy her drive.

So Sir Edmund and Sophie were free to ride off together, and if Sophie had not been worried about poor Priscilla's fate, she would have found the drive absolutely thrilling, as Sir Edmund was an expert at handling the ribbons and drove like the wind, though the hills surrounding Bath didn't always make it possible for him to go as fast as he would have liked. Still, this was a far more exciting ride than the only other one they'd had together, that excursion to Hyde Park so early in their acquaintance. This time Sophie could sit as close to him on the seat as she desired (and was encouraged to do so). The pace he set was not at all conducive to conversation, but they were able to exchange smiles and glances from time to time, and those looks contained a thousand things that mere words could not express anyway.

Sophie felt that there was a new openness and ease in his manner and wondered if this was what he had been like at nineteen, before that treacherous experience had made him unnaturally reserved and overly cautious. Or perhaps it was the knowledge that Sophie returned his regard that accounted for it. Whatever it was, Sophie was delighted that any restraint that had existed between them was now gone.

They had driven for about an hour when they approached the village of Corsham and Sir Edmund was obliged to slow his horses. "We could possibly catch up to them here at the posting inn. He'll need to change his team," he told her, and sure enough, when the Hare and Hounds came into sight, he triumphantly identified the post chaise pulled up there as the one he'd seen at the other inn earlier that morning.

A boy ran to the horses' heads as soon as Sir Edmund drove into the innyard, but Sophie stopped Sir Edmund with a hand on his sleeve when he was about to jump down from the curricle. "Please," she said, "let me speak to Priscilla alone. Perhaps she's had second thoughts and will be very willing to come back with us. And if she isn't," Sophie said, finishing her remark with a shrug, as it was clear that they could not force her and, as her husband was not there to do so, neither could they call Mr. Maitland to account.

Sir Edmund nodded his understanding but came around anyway to help Sophie down from the curricle.

Sophie walked over to the post chaise, hoping that Priscilla was inside and she would not have to go into the inn to search for her, while at the same time dreading the upcoming confrontation. She was relieved to find that there was a woman inside the carriage, but when she came face-to-face with her she was very surprised to see that it was *not* Priscilla Beswick.

17

⚬⟨∞⟩⟨∞⟩⚬

Charles Beswick returned to his lodgings and began throwing his things into a saddle bag, telling his manservant to pack up whatever was left in the house and to follow him to Devon.

"Except do not bring any of Mrs. Beswick's belongings. I do not want them. You can burn them, for all I care," he said, as he looked around him for anything he might have missed. As he was doing so he heard a door slam, followed by *her* voice.

"Charles? Where are you? I have a surprise for you," she called, as if nothing out of the ordinary was happening and she hadn't left him for another man.

"He's upstairs, Missus," Hitchens said, as he went down the stairs, "but he's not in the best of moods," Charles heard him say in a lowered tone of voice that was still perfectly audible.

"Charles!" she called again. "Come down as soon as you can. I have something to show you! Hitchens, come with me."

And then Charles heard her leave the house. It took him a moment to make sense of what was happening, but it slowly became obvious that if Priscilla was here . . . then she had *not* eloped with Maitland.

She had not eloped with Maitland!

Charles exited the town house to see Priscilla standing in front, dressed in the most exquisite dark blue riding habit he'd ever seen. And while it was very modest and covered her from chin to ankle, he couldn't help thinking it somehow emphasized her glorious figure more than any other costume she'd ever worn, particularly the braiding and frogging at her chest, to which his eyes kept returning. When he was finally able to draw them away, he noticed she was also wearing a tall shako hat with two huge white ostrich feathers. And, most surprisingly of all, she held the reins of the horse he had bought her as a wedding gift but which had been left in Devon.

"Well? Are you surprised? I sent Tom to Devon to bring Sugarplum to Bath"—Charles tried not to wince at what she'd insisted upon naming her horse—"and I commissioned the finest modiste in Bath to make me this habit so that we could go riding together. I actually had to go this morning at an ungodly hour for a final fitting just so it would be ready for me to wear today. There's a riding track around Sydney Gardens that I thought we could try, but if you want to ride further afield we can do so. Hitchens has gone to get *your* horse."

She was smiling at him, so very proud of herself for her surprise, and all he could think was that he had believed her to have been lost to him forever and so she had never seemed so precious. He grabbed her to him, kissing her as he'd never dared kiss her before, uncaring that they were standing in the street in full view of anyone who might happen by. She was surprised at first, but was soon kissing him back just as fervently, dropping the reins of her horse and sliding her hands around his neck as she attempted to press herself even closer to him. He realized he was probably destroying her grand outfit and that she cared about such things even if he did not, so he finally made himself pull away from her, though it pained him to do so. "Priscilla, we're going to ruin your hat," he said, straightening it, as he had disarranged it a little and it was no longer propped as saucily upon her head.

Priscilla just looked up at him, blinking, as if she did not know where she was. Finally she said, "Hang my hat," and pulled his head back down to hers.

They were eventually brought to their senses by Hitchens clearing his throat. He had Charles' horse saddled and was holding it ready for him, and he had also grabbed Sugarplum's reins, though Charles thought hazily that for once, riding a horse was the last activity he cared to participate in. He thought of another activity that appealed to him far more and smiled wickedly at Priscilla, a smile she returned, as if she knew exactly what he was thinking. Still, he couldn't very well ruin her big surprise, so he took some deep breaths and tried to calm himself.

"That is the loveliest getup I've ever seen you in," Charles said, in an attempt to change the subject, though the only conversation they'd been having had been happening in his head.

"Charles, was that a compliment?" Priscilla asked, her eyes opening wide. Charles thought they sparkled more than the finest emeralds and told her so.

"Is there an assembly this evening? I want to dance every dance with you," he said, and Priscilla could not believe this was really happening.

"Sophie is a genius," she said, and Hitchens thought this had to be the most nonsensical conversation he'd ever heard. "If we have a daughter we should name her Sophronia," Priscilla told Charles, "even though it's a horrible name."

"Whatever you want," Charles said.

Sophie, who was completely taken aback not to find Priscilla Beswick in the chaise, did not know what to say to explain herself to Lady Mary, who was the inhabitant of the carriage.

"I beg your pardon," Sophie said, but got no further. "Please excuse me," she tried again, and Lady Mary, who was an expert at filling awkward silences, chose this moment to remain mute. "May I just ask you, Lady Mary, if you're traveling with Mr. Maitland?" Sophie finally said, as

Frederick Maitland was not in the chaise with Lady Mary, and it occurred to Sophie that perhaps she had stumbled across the wrong carriage and Priscilla still needed to be rescued.

"I am. We are going to London, to be married," Lady Mary said, and Sophie did her best not to appear shocked, as she realized that would be very insulting to Lady Mary.

"I wish you both . . . all the happiness in the world," Sophie said, and Lady Mary nodded regally in response. Sophie began backing away from the chaise, intent now upon reaching the curricle before she had an even more awkward meeting with Frederick Maitland. As soon as she was out of sight of the carriage she ran the rest of the way to the curricle, telling Sir Edmund hurriedly, "Let us go; it is not Priscilla. She must still be in Bath. Hurry, before Mr. Maitland sees us."

And Sir Edmund drove quickly out of the innyard, just as Frederick Maitland exited the inn.

As soon as they had left the village behind them, Sophie explained to Sir Edmund who was in the carriage.

"Lady Mary?" he repeated incredulously, and Sophie couldn't help feeling sorry for her, as this was likely to be the universal response to the news of her marriage. "I can't believe it! It seemed completely in character for him to run off with Priscilla Beswick for a temporary liaison, but if he wished to marry someone I was sure he would ask *you*."

"Yes, well, he did propose, the day after we were at Newbrooke, but I declined his offer."

"Sophie! You refused him even before you'd had my

letter," Sir Edmund said, letting his horses slow to a walk while he stole a quick kiss. "You don't know how pleased I am to hear it. I couldn't help feeling a little jealous of him, as he was your first love."

"As to that, it's a good thing you did write me that letter, because when he proposed and I didn't accept he correctly deduced I had feelings for you and told me the story of what happened at Cambridge, but painted *you* as the villain of the piece."

"I'm not surprised. He would have done anything to win you. I could almost feel sorry for him, if he weren't such a fool."

They rode in silence for a moment, as Sophie considered Mr. Maitland's unusual choice of wife. "He married for money before, but perhaps this time his motive *was* unselfish. His children are fond of Lady Mary. And he told me she reminded him of his first wife," she said.

"Ha! He married her because she's connected to every noble family in England," Sir Edmund said.

"But they're eloping, which means Lady Smallpeace must not have given her permission for the match. Lady Mary's connections will do him no good if she's cut from society."

"Lady Smallpeace will come around. Maitland's an expert at twisting women around his little finger," he said bitterly.

Sophie looked at him with a mischievous smile. "It sounds as if you're more than a *little* jealous."

Sir Edmund saw a wide section of road ahead and steered the curricle to one side, bringing the horses to a halt before pulling Sophie into his arms. "*He* is the one who should be jealous of *me*," he said, kissing her. He pulled back to look at her face, running a finger over her cheek, which was softer than any rose petal. "And I'm very sure he is, the poor dastard."

There was an assembly that evening, and Sir Edmund, Sophie, Mrs. Foster, Cecilia, and the Beswicks were all in attendance. Priscilla told Sophie that she was brilliant, her best friend in the entire world, and that she was naming her unborn daughter after her, before asking: "Do you have a second name?"

"No, I'm afraid not," Sophie said. "I think my parents thought 'Sophronia Lattimore' was long enough."

Priscilla sighed. "That's a great pity."

Charles Beswick had not stopped smiling the entire evening and Sophie thought his facial muscles were likely to be sore, as they were so unused to assuming such a position. He approached her at one point to thank her for her help, and Sophie asked him, with a teasing smile, if they were to see him in the Pump Room the next day.

"Not tomorrow, as Priscilla has planned for us to walk Beechen Cliff. But if she wants to go to the Pump Room the morning after I will happily escort her."

"You are to stay in Bath, then?"

"For a few weeks at least. It feels more like a honeymoon here than our original one did," Charles said.

Sophie strongly doubted the honeymoon would last that long—she was sure the tempestuous young couple would find something else to argue about before the week was out—but she felt that at least they had learned to more deeply value each other and to find enjoyment in activities and pursuits together. Watching them that evening, Sophie noticed that Charles Beswick was a remarkably good dancer and appeared to like it very much, and when Sophie asked Priscilla if she was enjoying participating with Charles in *his* favorite activities, Priscilla blushed a fiery red and said, "Oh, yes!" very fervently. At which point Sophie decided it was best not to probe into the affairs of a newly married couple *too* closely and changed the subject.

Emily Woodford was also present that evening, but there was an awkwardness between her and Sophie now that nothing could overcome, and they did no more than exchange distant nods. At any other time Sophie would have been sorry that their friendship had come to such an abrupt end, but she was far too happy over her engagement to allow it to depress her tonight, though she did feel a pang of sympathy for Emily, who must have heard that Mr. Hartwell had left town and realized he was lost to her.

The only existing worry Sophie had was over Cecilia. Cecilia had a number of invitations to dance, which she accepted politely, and she was careful to smile and even to laugh, but there was no denying she was unhappy. Sophie knew she missed Mr. Hartwell, whether or not she was sure she loved him. Sophie was watching Cecilia dance, a pensive expression on her face, when Edmund spoke in her ear.

"You have a very determined glint in your eye as you survey those unsuspecting couples. I hope you're not planning any more matches," he said.

Sophie turned and smiled up at him. "I am not, I promise you. I am too consumed with joy over the excellent match I made for myself."

"Do you mean to say I was the target of a scheming matchmaker all along and wasn't even aware of it?"

"You were. However, there was nothing for you to fear, because this particular matchmaker is very bad at scheming."

"You're right, you know. You're incapable of artifice. It's one of the things I love about you," Edmund said, lowering his voice even more, and Sophie felt a delicious thrill.

"This is quite the most interesting conversation I've had all evening," she said, opening her fan and hiding the bottom half of her face behind it. "Tell me what else you love about me," she said, dropping her own voice to a whisper.

"I'd far rather show you," he whispered back, and she looked around to make sure no one was observing them, because she was quite sure his lips had brushed her ear while he was speaking.

He then began stroking the bare skin above the back of her dress, his hand cleverly positioned where no one could see it, and she wondered how a man who had avoided her sex for so many years had become so very accomplished so quickly.

"Who taught you to flirt, Sir Edmund?" she asked somewhat breathlessly. "You're quite skilled at the art."

"The most adorable, delectable woman of my acquaintance," he said. "My heart, my love, my Sophie."

18

A few days later Cecilia and Sophie were walking on Milsom Street when a sedan chair pulled up next to them, seemingly in a great rush. Both the men who were carrying the chair, one in front and one in back, were jogging and breathing heavily. Cecilia and Sophie stepped out of the way, thinking the carriers would hurry past them, but instead their passenger hissed at them.

"Pssst, Miss Foster," a man said, and looking inside the box, Cecilia realized it was Lord Courtney. She did not know if he expected her to speak to him while he was being carried by two other men, but after a moment he instructed them to let him out of the chair. Cecilia, exchanging a puzzled glance with Sophie, waited for him to exit.

"Frightfully warm day for a walk, is it not?" he eventually said, after having paid the chairmen and watched them leave.

Cecilia thought this was an unusual way to start the conversation, as he had not, in fact, been walking. Thankfully he didn't wait for a reply but, turning to address Sophie, continued: "Miss Lattimore, I have something to discuss in private with Miss Foster, if you wouldn't mind . . ."

He let his sentence trail off as he looked at her expectantly, and Sophie wondered what he expected her to do to facilitate his privacy with Cecilia. They were standing in the middle of Milsom Street; where did he expect her to go? Was she supposed to walk off and leave her cousin with him, and then be left to walk alone herself? Finally she just replied, "I do not mind if you speak to Miss Foster."

This appeared to satisfy him, as he offered Cecilia his arm and began to walk with her, and Sophie followed them, a pace or two behind.

"Miss Foster," he said, in a conspiratorial tone Sophie imagined he thought was lowered, but since he fairly yelled every time he spoke, what he said was still perfectly audible to Sophie and anyone else within ten feet. "I imagine you heard my cousin eloped with Maitland. As distasteful as that is for a woman of her age," he said with a slight shudder, "it actually made me think about doing something similar. And Miss Foster—or Cecily, if I may be so bold—"

"Cecilia," Cecilia corrected him.

"What?"

"My name is Cecilia," she said.

"And *you* may call *me* Court," he told her. "Celia, my

darling, my aunt would never consent to our marriage, so we'll just have to make a dash to the border."

"I am sorry, Lord Courtney—"

"Court," he reminded her.

"Um, Court, you do me great honor," she began again, "but I'm afraid we would not suit."

"There's nothing to be afraid of, my dear Celia, I don't care if you had whooping cough at twelve and your great-uncle *was* a yeoman farmer. You suit me down to the ground," he said. "I'd show you right now how well we suit if your pesky cousin wasn't so close by." He looked over his shoulder at Sophie as he said this, who felt she'd heard more than enough and came forward.

"Lord Courtney, Cecilia is not running off to Gretna Green with you, so you'll have to find some other young woman to delight with your attentions."

He looked Sophie up and down. "I'm sure you'd like that," he said, winking salaciously at her.

Sophie and Cecilia locked arms and began walking away from Lord Courtney.

"I won't ask you again—this is your only chance!" he yelled after them. "Cecily!"

The Foster ladies had decided to extend their visit to Bath and made plans to stay until after Sophie's wedding, as they were situated so close to Newbrooke and the wedding was being held in the parish church there, and Sophie couldn't very well stay in Bath without them. The engagement announcement had been printed in the papers, the first of the banns was read that Sunday, and a wedding date was set for the following month. Sophie frequently found herself wondering if it was all really happening, and thanked God that Mr. Maitland *had* jilted her all those years ago. She found it so strange the incident she had considered the most tragic and ruinous of her life she now considered a great blessing, and she realized just how limited her perspective—and any person's—really was.

Such considerations made her more determined than ever not to interfere in her cousin's romance, because who was to say whether, with the benefit of hindsight, Cecilia or even Mr. Hartwell might one day congratulate themselves on the wisdom of *their* parting when they had.

Though Cecilia was obviously very depressed over Mr. Hartwell's absence, she put forth her best efforts to act cheerful, even though Sophie realized it probably made Cecilia conscious of her own loss when she participated in Sophie and Edmund's engagement festivities. Still, Sophie told herself again and again, she could not, would not, get involved.

And she most definitely would not write Mr. Hartwell a letter.

However, someone else took it upon themselves to write to him, and a month after his departure from Bath he returned, much to the surprise of the inhabitants of number 4 Rivers Street.

Sophie's wedding was in three days and the ladies had

just returned from a trip to Newbrooke, so had made no plans for the evening but were sitting together in the drawing room. The clock had just struck nine and they were certainly not expecting callers, but Mr. Hartwell burst into the room even before Jonas could announce him and quickly ran over to Cecilia, throwing himself at her feet and grabbing her hand.

"Cecilia! Thank God! I was afraid I would be too late!"

Jonas appeared in the doorway and looked at Mrs. Foster as if to ask should he throw Mr. Hartwell out, but Mrs. Foster gave a little shake of her head and Jonas withdrew.

Mr. Hartwell did look half-crazed, and the ladies would have been surprised by his sudden appearance anyway, as they thought him in Derbyshire, but all were shocked even further by the sight of the normally placid Mr. Hartwell in the grip of such strong emotion. Nor was he dressed for a social call; he was still in his traveling clothes, and it appeared as if he had come directly there upon his arrival in town.

"Too late?" Cecilia asked, and Sophie noticed she did not withdraw her hand from his but let go of her sewing to offer him her other hand as well.

"I had no idea—why did you not tell me? Cecilia, my love!" he said incoherently, before suddenly pulling her to his chest in a tight embrace.

Mrs. Foster's eyes were nearly popping out of her head, and Sophie was quite shocked as well, as she had never seen such behavior in a polite drawing room (though she and Sir Edmund had grown quite adept at finding other, more private locations for very similar behavior since their betrothal). Still, she did not think Edmund would ever attempt to embrace her in the presence of her relations, nor did she desire him to.

"Mr. Hartwell!" Mrs. Foster said, her ringing tones bringing him to an awareness of what he was doing.

"I beg your pardon, Mrs. Foster, but I was told—" He looked at Cecilia again and, as if he could not prevent himself from touching her, clasped her cheek in his hand. "You are pale, my love. How are you feeling? Are you in any pain?"

And Sophie finally realized what it was he'd been told and could have laughed at the result of her aunt's little fib, if it were not obvious that Mr. Hartwell had been deeply pained by it.

Cecilia had obviously reached the same conclusion as Sophie. "Laurence," she said in a soft voice, before lightly kissing the hand that held her face, "I am fine. I am perfectly healthy. It is just a rumor. You have nothing to fear."

And Mr. Hartwell took a deep, shuddering breath before drawing Cecilia back into his arms and kissing her as if *his* life depended on it.

Sophie and Mrs. Foster exchanged a look and then, by mutual unspoken consent, left the drawing room.

The couple who were kissing on the sofa did not even notice their departure, but eventually they broke apart long enough to offer each other explanations and avowals.

"I was so stupid; how can you bear to have anything to do with me?" Cecilia asked.

"Don't say such things about yourself! You're just young; I shouldn't have been so impatient with you. You can take all the time you need," he told her, as he continued to press kisses upon her. Which had the effect of making Cecilia think that waiting longer than necessary to marry was a terrible waste of time indeed.

"It is just—I met you first, instead of last, you see," Cecilia said, trying to explain her wretched folly in taking so long to recognize his worth. And with this incoherent explanation Laurence Hartwell was perfectly satisfied, and indeed, he had no right to complain of his beloved's lack of eloquence, because he was making absolutely no sense himself.

It was a sunny day in September when Sophie Lattimore took Sir Edmund Winslow to wedded husband. Cecilia was the one bridesmaid and, as a newly engaged woman soon to marry the man she loved, looked almost as radiant as the bride.

But no woman could outshine Sophie that day. She was wearing an original design by Priscilla Beswick, a white satin slip with an overskirt of lamé shot through with silver threads, and she literally sparkled. She wore no cap or bonnet, but an aigrette of pearls pulled her hair back from her forehead, and white roses that Edmund had given her were placed here and there in her dark curls. The scent wafted up to Edmund as he stood by her side at the altar, and he was reminded of a stolen kiss taken in a garden bower and formed the resolve to kiss the new Lady Winslow in the same spot as soon as it could be arranged.

When the vicar came to the part of the service that stated

holy matrimony was not to be taken "wantonly, to satisfy men's carnal lusts and appetites," Edmund winked at Sophie and she had to suppress a giggle. She would have laughed outright if she had seen how her aunt glared at Mr. Hartwell, who had been under constant surveillance since his overly affectionate behavior when he thought Cecilia was dying. The poor couple were allowed very little privacy, and Cecilia, who had once been so hesitant to marry Laurence Hartwell, was now suggesting he purchase a special license so they did not have to wait for the banns to be called.

Lord Fitzwalter was Sir Edmund's best man, and Charles and Priscilla Beswick were also in attendance, and they all stayed for the wedding breakfast held at Newbrooke after the ceremony. Everyone was in the best of spirits (even before imbibing them), and once the cake was cut, Lord Fitzwalter began the toasting by suggesting they all drink to the bride.

"To Sophie, Lady Winslow, we wish for you all that you deserve: the happiest of marriages with an affectionate, generous, and indulgent husband," Fitzwalter said, nodding and winking at Sir Edmund, "good friends, and excellent health! To Lady Winslow!"

"To Lady Cupid! To Sophie!" the guests shouted. And Sophie, looking around the room at the faces of her dear friends, family, and her beloved husband, was so very glad she had written that letter.

London, Thursday (April 10, 1817)

Lord Fitzwalter,

Please forgive my impudence in writing to you; I would not have taken such a task upon myself if I did not think it was of the utmost importance and could have a direct bearing upon your future happiness.

It is common knowledge in London society that you have been courting Miss Priscilla Hammond, and while she seems an admirable young lady, I have reason to believe that she is in love with another gentleman and that they have made promises to each other. It also appears that her mother has been strongly encouraging her to accept your addresses because of the title and estate you hold. On the other hand, it has also come to my attention that Miss Lucy Barrett, the sister of one of your dear friends, is truly and sincerely enamored of you, and has chosen you based on nothing other than the leadings of a pure and tender heart, untainted by any mercenary motives or considerations of social rank. She loves you for yourself alone, and it is my opinion that each of us could desire nothing more than to find that person who believes us as wonderful as we aspire to be. Since I myself have no likelihood of finding such a precious gift, it pains me all the more to see one who has it within his grasp fail to obtain it. It is for this reason that I have written you this letter.

Your sincere well-wisher,
An anonymous lady

Acknowledgments

I don't know if you all remember the year 2020, but it was a dark time to write a light, romantic comedy. I found it creatively challenging for many reasons, but it was especially difficult having to stay inside my tiny house (which seemed to get smaller as the months wore on) day in and day out, with no trips to the locations I was writing about, or even to a local coffee shop, to do research and gather inspiration.

So, I'd like to thank my husband Jonathan for being a great person with whom to be stuck inside during a global pandemic, as well as a terrific cook. If I hadn't already dedicated my last book to him, this one would have been dedicated to him as well.

Thanks also to my editor, Kate Seaver, for being such a pleasant and lovely person, as well as having great suggestions; and my agent, Stefanie Lieberman, who is always so responsive, knowledgeable, and helpful. Stefanie and Kate also had much to contend with during 2020 but remained professional, patient, and cooperative. Thank you, Kate and Stefanie!

I also greatly appreciate the help of Kirsten Elliott, who arranged for me to get a digital copy of her book: *No Swinging on Sundays: The Story of Bath's Lost Pleasure Gardens*. Although I was unable to travel physically to Bath while writing this novel, her meticulously researched book took me there—and to Sydney Gardens in particular—as well as taking me back in time.

Finally, to the sisters I mentioned in my dedication: Charlotte, who arranged for a virtual celebration of my twenty-fifth wedding anniversary while under lockdown, and Vicky, who checks in on me every day and helps me care for our parents; thank you for always being awesome and supportive sisters. And to my other sisters, who may not be physically related to me but whom I love just as much: Kimberly, Walsta, Wanyda, Deniece, De, Michelle, Amber, Marianne, Denise, Tammy, Karrie, Nakia, Nekia, Keren, Rongmei, Ryann, Summer, Jen, Jan, Genevieve, Melissa, Carol, Rachel, Tiffany, Melinda, Pam, Debi, Leslie, Kayshauna, and Alesheia: I'm so grateful for you all! And I know there's probably someone super special I didn't include, so just insert your name here: _____. I have so many supportive, loving, beautiful friends. I am truly blessed. (A special thanks to Alison, too, for being one of the first to read *Miss Lattimore's Letter* and for sharing your impressions with me. It's a good thing you liked it!)

Suzanne Allain is a screenwriter who lived in New York and Beijing before returning to her hometown of Tallahassee, Florida, where she lives with her husband. She makes frequent visits to Los Angeles for work, but one of her most memorable trips was to London to see her script *Mr. Malcolm's List: Overture* being filmed.

Ready to find
your next great read?

Let us help.

Visit prh.com/nextread

Penguin
Random
House